This House Had Always Been Ali's Home, Her Refuge. Yet Now, As She Moved From Room To Room, She Felt Nothing But Emptiness.

She blamed her sadness on being forced to leave. But she knew the true cause of it was the man who had briefly shared the house with her.

The scent of him still hung in her bedroom, a reminder of that first night he'd come to her there. And when she curled up to sleep, she envisioned him braced above her there, in her bed.

She shrugged away the troubling thoughts and went back to packing.

And if she had to wipe away an occasional tear, she blamed it on the dust she was stirring up. It certainly wasn't because she was missing Garrett Miller.

She told herself she hadn't fallen in love with him, but she had—and he'd deceived her.

Dear Reader,

At long last the final book in my A PIECE OF TEXAS series. This story centers on Ali Moran—twin sister of Jase Calhoun, the hero from *The Texan's Secret Past*— and Garrett Miller, founder and owner of Future Concepts, a billion-dollar computer company. Their story opens on the first day of January, the perfect time for all new beginnings. Ali and Garrett are the epitome of the odd couple, as she is creative, warm and friendly, and he is…well, he's a geek. A wealthy and handsome geek, but a geek nonetheless.

January is one of my favorite months—and not because of the weather! I really, really *hate* being cold! But I do like what January represents. For me, it's a new beginning, a chance to reevaluate my life and steer it in the direction I want it to take making any necessary changes—as well as a few resolutions I may or may not keep.

I hope you enjoy this last book in my series, and I hope you'll take the time to jot down a few resolutions of your own for the New Year. And make sure the first one is to fill your year with romance!

Happy New Year!

Peggy

THE TEXAN'S CONTESTED CLAIM

PEGGY MORELAND

Published by Silhouette Books

America's Publisher of Contemporary Romance

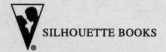 SILHOUETTE BOOKS

ISBN-13: 978-0-373-76844-8
ISBN-10:   0-373-76844-3

THE TEXAN'S CONTESTED CLAIM

PEGGY MORELAND

published her first romance with Silhouette Books in 1989 and continues to delight readers with stories set in her home state of Texas. Peggy is a winner of a National Readers' Choice Award, a nominee for *Romantic Times BOOKreviews* Reviewer's Choice Award and a two-time finalist for a prestigious RITA® Award, and her books frequently appear on the *USA TODAY* and Waldenbooks's bestseller lists. When not writing, Peggy can usually be found outside, tending the cattle, goats and other critters on the ranch she shares with her husband. You may write to Peggy at P.O. Box 1099, Florence, TX 76527-1099, or e-mail her at peggy@peggymoreland.com.

Without avid readers, where would an author be?
Over the last eighteen-plus years, I've received thousands
of letters and e-mails from readers all over the world,
who were kind enough to take the time to write
and tell me how much they enjoy my books.
To each and every one of you, I dedicate this book.

One

To Garrett Miller, timing was everything, both in business and in life.

And the timing on his trip to Austin, Texas, couldn't be more perfect.

His number one goal in making the trip was to reunite his stepmother with Ali Moran, the daughter she'd given up for adoption thirty years prior. If that failed, he intended to persuade—or coerce, if necessary—Ali to give him the missing portion of the deed she held, which would enable his stepmother and her new husband to fulfill the requirements to claim a ranch they had been given.

As fate would have it, he also needed to locate

property for an expansion he was planning for his company. Since Austin was quickly establishing itself as the Silicon Valley of the Southwest, it seemed the natural choice and gave him the perfect excuse to make the trip.

The kick was, he had to accomplish it all without anyone discovering he was in Austin.

Scowling, he punched in the code for the electronic gate of Vista Bed and Breakfast, given to his secretary when she booked his reservation. If he'd known success would make him so damn popular with the media, he would've remained a geek for the rest of his life and never started Future Concepts. Who would've thought the public would care about a businessman's every move?

Or that success would make him a target for some crazy who wanted him dead?

He shoved the disturbing thought from his mind as he drove through the open gates. As far as the rest of the world was concerned, he reminded himself, Garrett Miller was currently attending a technology seminar in Switzerland, a lie his public relations department had fed the media at his request. All Garrett had to do was keep his presence in Austin under wraps, and his stalker would follow the bait to Switzerland and hopefully fall right into the trap being set for him there.

Pulling up in front of the two-story home, he

parked the rental car he'd picked up at the airport,
then leaned across the seat to peer up at the house.
He studied the structure a long moment, thinking of
the woman inside, as well as his chances of gaining
her cooperation. He'd given himself a month to find
a way to convince her to reunite with his stepmother,
though he doubted it would take anywhere near that
long. Everyone had a price—or a weakness. It was
just a matter of discovering Ali's.

He smiled smugly as he climbed from the car. He
didn't doubt for a minute he'd succeed. Knowledge
was power and, thanks to the P.I. he'd hired and the
research he'd done on his own, he knew all there was
to know about Ali Moran.

And she knew virtually nothing about him.

Perched high on a ladder, Ali stretched to snag the
last ornament from the Christmas tree's uppermost
branch. In spite of the cheery fire burning in the
fireplace and her favorite Norah Jones CD playing
on the stereo, she couldn't have worked up a smile
if she had wanted to. January 1 was usually her
favorite day of the year—sleeping late after celebrat-
ing the New Year with her friends, eating a huge
bowl of black-eyed peas for good luck, making a list
of resolutions she wouldn't keep. Best of all,
January 1 marked the first day of her annual four-
week vacation.

But there would be no vacation for Ali this year.

Grimacing, she tucked the ornament into the box and started down the ladder. It was her own fault, she told herself. She'd let greed get the best of her.

And who wouldn't? she asked herself in frustration. When a zillionaire calls you up and offers you four times the going rate to reserve your entire bed-and-breakfast for a month, it's kind of hard to say no. Cooking and cleaning for *one* guest, rather than the five her B&B was designed to accommodate, and getting paid four times the money for her trouble? Only a fool would turn down a deal as sweet as that.

"So quit your whining," she lectured, as she stooped to place the box of ornaments in a storage crate. The money she would earn far outweighed whatever sacrifices were required of her, including giving up her vacation.

Grimacing, she slapped the crate's flaps into place. "But that doesn't mean I have to like it," she grumbled under her breath.

The doorbell rang and she straightened with a frown. Who on earth would drop by this early in the morning on New Year's Day? she wondered. Everyone she knew would still be in bed, after partying all night—which is exactly where she'd be, if she wasn't expecting a guest to arrive that afternoon.

At the thought of her guest, she caught her lower lip between her teeth. Surely he hadn't arrived early.

She'd specifically told him check-in time wasn't until three. But who else could it be? Unable to think of a soul who'd be up and about this early on New Year's Day, she started grabbing decorations and shoving them into boxes, mortified at the thought of inviting *anyone* into her home with it looking such a mess, much less Garrett Miller.

The bell sounded a second time, setting her teeth on edge. Dropping the evergreen swag she held, she marched for the front door, telling herself he could just deal, since he had chosen to ignore check-in time.

At the door, she paused to drag the elastic band from her hair and stole a peek through the peephole. She blinked, blinked again. If she hadn't already checked out her guest on the Internet, she might not have recognized the man standing on her porch as the owner of a world-renowned company like Future Concepts. Dressed in faded jeans, a worn leather jacket and aviator sunglasses, he looked too…well, *normal*.

The bell rang a third time, making her jump. She blew out a breath, then pasted on a cheerful smile and swung open the door.

"Hi," she said and extended her hand in greeting. "You must be Garrett. I'm Ali, the innkeeper of Vista Bed and Breakfast."

He stared, the oddest expression coming over his face, but didn't make a move to take her hand.

She took a closer look at him. "You *are* Garrett Miller, aren't you?"

The question seemed to snap him from his trance-like state.

"Sorry," he said and took her hand. "It's just that you look very much like…someone I know."

A tingle of awareness skittered up her arm as his fingers closed around hers. Surprised by the sensation—and not at all sure she liked it—she broke the connection.

"You know what they say," she said, with a careless shrug. "Everyone has a twin."

He got that odd look on his face again and she inwardly groaned, thinking it was going to be a *very* long month.

"Come on in," she said and opened the door wider. "You'll have to pardon the mess," she warned, thinking it best to prepare him for the disaster that awaited them in the den. "You caught me in the middle of clearing away my Christmas decorations."

He stepped past her, trailing the seductive scent of sandalwood in his wake. "I hope my arriving early isn't an inconvenience. I had my pilot fly me in earlier than I'd originally planned."

He had his own pilot? Which probably meant he had his own plane, too. Unable to imagine that kind of wealth or the freedom it offered, she swallowed an envious sigh. "No problem." She glanced out the door toward the rental car parked in her driveway. "Do you need help with your luggage?"

He pulled off his sunglasses, looking around as he tucked them into the inside pocket of his jacket. "I'll get it later, if that's all right."

When he met her gaze again, sans the sunglasses, she felt that same tingle of awareness she'd experienced when he'd clasped her hand, only this time he hadn't touched her.

"Oh, wow," she breathed, finding it all but impossible to look away.

"Excuse me?"

"Your eyes," she said. "I didn't notice until you took off your glasses. They're brown. That rich, dark, melted chocolate kind of brown. And when the light hits them just right—" she opened and closed the door, varying the amount of light striking his face "—these little gold flecks flash like tiny explosions of light."

He reached inside his jacket. "I can put them back on, if it bothers you."

Realizing she was making a fool of herself, she offered him a sheepish smile. "Sorry," she said, as she closed the door. "I tend to get carried away about lighting. It's one of the curses of being a photographer. This way," she said, and motioned for him to follow her. "I'll give you a quick tour of the downstairs, then take you up to your room.

"Formal living room and dining room," she said, gesturing left and right as she moved down the hall. "You're welcome to use both, but most of my guests prefer the coziness of the den and breakfast room at the rear of the house. There's a beautiful view of Town Lake through the windows there."

She paused to point to a closed door at the end of a short hall. "That's the entrance to my private living quarters. It's the only portion of the house that's off-limits to guests."

He stopped beside her. "I noticed on your Web site that you cater to businessmen." He angled his head to peer at her. "I believe the blurb read something like, 'the Vista, where *all* the needs of the corporate traveler are met.'"

The emphasis he placed on "all," as well as his suggestive tone, put Ali's back up. "If you're thinking the Vista is a front for a call girl service," she informed him tersely, "you're wrong."

"I didn't say it was," he returned mildly.

"Well, just so you understand, I provide my clients with nothing more than comfortable accommodations, home-cooked meals and workspace should they need it."

"Which is all I expect," he assured her. "I was merely curious why a woman who lives alone would prefer men as guests."

She narrowed her eyes. "I never said I lived alone."

"You didn't have to. Your repeated use of 'my' and 'I' made it obvious."

When she continued to eye him suspiciously, he dropped his hands to his hips, and the corners of his mouth into a frown.

"Look," he said, clearly irritated with her. "If you're worried about your safety, don't be. You're perfectly safe with me. I'm not interested in you *or* your body. And just so *you* understand," he said, tossing her own words back at her, "if and when I'm in the mood for female companionship, I sure as hell don't need someone to arrange it for me."

She wasn't sure whether to be relieved or insulted, but one thing was certain—she'd angered her guest…something a person in her business couldn't afford to do.

"I'm sorry," she said, and meant it. "I'm usually not this defensive."

"And I'm not usually mistaken for a predator," he snapped back at her.

She squinched up her nose. "Can we hit Rewind?" she asked hopefully. "It seems we've gotten off to a bad start."

"If it makes you feel better thinking our relationship will improve by starting over—" he tossed up a hand "—then by all means consider the tape rewound."

To prove her willingness to play nice, she forced a smile. "Thanks. And to answer your question about my preference for business travelers, this is my home, as well as a bed-and-breakfast, and I discovered early on that businessmen are less disruptive to my daily life than tourists. Since they generally book only on weekdays, that's an advantage, too, as it leaves my weekends free for my other job."

He lifted a brow. "Other job?"

"Photography. I'm an aspiring photojournalist."

"A woman of many talents."

"You might want to withhold judgment until you see my work," she warned, then smiled again and motioned him to follow her. "Come on, let's finish the tour."

She started down the hall again toward the kitchen. "In the mornings, you'll find juice and coffee on the buffet in the breakfast room. I normally serve breakfast at seven on weekdays and eight on weekends, but since you're my only guest, you can choose a different time, if you like."

"Your current schedule is fine."

"The den is through here," she said, and led the way through an arched doorway. She stopped, her shoulders sagging at the amount of work awaiting her. "Welcome to the after-Christmas nightmare," she said wearily.

"Damn," he murmured, staring, then glanced her way. "Do you decorate every room in the house?"

"Pretty much. My friends accuse me of trying to make up for my dismal childhood Christmases."

"Dismal?"

"A tabletop Christmas tree and one present dispensed on Christmas Eve just before bedtime."

"Were your parents poor?"

She choked a laugh. "Hardly. More like boring." Doubting her guest was interested in hearing about her dysfunctional family, she pointed to the antique armoire, all but concealed by the wreaths stacked high in front. "Believe it or not, there's a flat screen television hiding behind that pile of greenery. You're welcome to watch TV here or in your room, whichever you prefer. I have a wireless network, so you can connect to the Internet anywhere inside the house, as well as the patios outside.

"Both the front and back doors have a keyless entry," she went on to explain. "I change the code every couple of weeks for security purposes. That's about it downstairs," she said and gestured toward a set of stairs on the far side of the room. "We'll take the rear staircase to the second floor."

When she reached the top landing, she headed for the opposite end of the hall. "You can have your pick of the bedrooms," she told him, "but since you're staying a month, I think the suite will better suit your needs. It has a separate sitting room, with a minifridge and bar. Plus, the bathroom is larger than the others, and has a tub perfect for soaking— a bonus, if you enjoy taking long baths."

She pushed open the door to the suite then stepped back out of the way. "Unless you have any questions, I'll leave you to settle in."

"Just one."

"What?"

"When my secretary made my reservations, she asked that you keep my stay here confidential."

She held her hand up like a good Girl Scout. "I haven't told a soul."

"Good. No one can know I'm here."

She teased him with a smile. "Why? Are the cops after you?"

He seemed to hesitate a moment, then shook his head. "No. I'm here to check out locations for a future expansion for my company. It's imperative that my presence, as well as my plans, remain secret until I'm ready to go public."

She drew an imaginary zipper across her mouth. "Your secret is safe with me. Anything else?"

"Not at the moment."

"Well, if you think of something, I'll be in the den dealing with the ghost of Christmas past."

Garrett shook his head as he crossed to the bathroom to put away his shaving kit, unable to believe how close he'd come to blowing his cover. When Ali had opened the door to greet him, her likeness to his stepmother had momentarily rendered him speechless. The same blond hair and blue eyes, the same delicate features. They even had similar mannerisms, which he found inconceivable, since the two had never met.

He'd almost slipped and told her his reason for staring, and would have if he hadn't been distracted by the jolt he'd received when he'd taken her hand. He'd seen the surprise that had flared in her eyes, sensed her unease in the quickness with which she had broken the contact, and knew she must have felt it, too.

He thought he'd done a decent job of recovering, then she'd made that comment about everybody having a twin and thrown him for another loop. If she hadn't appeared so genuinely guileless, he might have thought she was purposely trying to trip him up. As it was, he believed he'd successfully penetrated the enemy's camp.

Penetrated the enemy's camp?

Snorting a laugh, he tossed his shaving kit onto the vanity. Hell, he was even beginning to *think* in the vernacular of a spy.

With a rueful shake of his head, he turned for the bedroom, but stopped when he caught a glimpse of the tub she'd mentioned. Placed on a raised platform of tumbled stone tiles, it resembled an old-fashioned claw-foot in design, but its size and modern fixtures placed it solidly in the twenty-first century.

Remembering her comment about the tub being

perfect for soaking, he crossed to examine it more closely. It definitely looked inviting, he noted, with its extra long length and gently sloped ends. He glanced up at the large picture window above it. And the uninterrupted view of lake and sky it offered its occupant wasn't too shabby, either, he noted. Personally he preferred a shower, but he could see how a person might enjoy taking a long, relaxing bath in a setup like this. Add a woman to the mix and even *he* might be persuaded to forego a shower for a bath.

He squinted his eyes at the view beyond the window, easily able to imagine the scene at night. Moonlight reflecting off the lake's surface. A sky full of glittering stars. Toss in some soft piano music and a mountain of scented bubbles and it would provide the perfect setting for a seduction.

He dropped his gaze to the tub again, wondering if the Vista's innkeeper ever took advantage of the amenities the bath offered when she had the house all to herself. She seemed the bubble-bath type. Feminine. Sensual. In fact, he found it easy to picture her here, her head tipped back against the tub's rolled rim, her eyes closed, only her knees and head visible above mounds of iridescent bubbles.

Even easier—and a great deal more pleasurable— was to picture her there with *him*.

Puckering his lips thoughtfully, he dragged a finger along the rim, imagining them in the tub together, her back against his chest, her hips wedged between his thighs, his hands tracing her curves. She was stacked. He'd made that realization within seconds of her opening the door. And she had a mouth made for kissing. Full, moist lips that seemed curved in an ever-present smile.

With one memorable exception.

He chuckled softly, as he recalled her indignation when he'd insinuated the bed-and-breakfast was a front for a call girl service. She'd assumed correctly. He had thought, hoped even, that she was using the bed-and-breakfast as a front for illegal activities.

Too bad he'd been wrong, he thought with regret. If he'd been right, it would have provided him the leverage he needed to force her cooperation.

It also would have given him more reason to dislike Ali Moran.

Not that he needed more cause.

The hurt she'd inflicted on his stepmother was reason enough to wish her in hell.

Two

"Traci!" Ali shot a worried glance up at the ceiling, then lowered her gaze to frown at her laughing friend. "Get a grip, would you? He might hear you."

Traci winced guiltily. "Sorry. But when you said that about the Vista being a front for a call girl service, I had this mental image of you strutting around in skin-hugging spandex and spike heels. Can you imagine? You, a madam? Or worse, a call girl? What a hoot!"

"I could be a call girl," Ali said defensively. "Not that I ever would, but I *could*."

"Are you kidding me?" Traci said in dismay. "If

you had to depend on turning tricks for your support, you'd starve to death within a week."

Grimacing, Ali yanked open the oven door. "Well, thanks for that vote of confidence," she groused, as she shoved a basket of sopaipillas inside to keep warm.

Traci managed to snag a pastry before Ali could close the oven door. "I'm not saying you couldn't *attract* a man," she said, as she spooned honey into the pastry's puffed center. "But there's more to being a call girl than wearing skimpy clothes and flashing cleavage."

Ali gave her a bland look. "Oh, and I suppose you're an expert on the subject."

"I watch enough cop shows to teach a course. And let me tell you," she went on, warming to the subject, "the hookers they haul off the streets aren't particular about who they have sex with. They can't afford to be. *You,* on the other hand, would turn up your nose at the slightest physical flaw."

Ali's jaw dropped. "Are you saying I'm a sexual snob?"

Traci caught a dribble of honey on the tip of her finger and brought it to her mouth. "Need I remind you of Richard?"

Ali shuddered at the mention of the C.P.A. she'd briefly dated. "Please. Just thinking about his clammy hands and slobbery kisses makes me want to hurl."

"And you think the men call girls entertain are Brad Pitt lookalikes?"

"Okay, okay," Ali grumbled. "You made your point."

Traci smiled smugly. "I so love it when I'm right."

"Shh," Ali hissed, and listened, sure that she'd heard footsteps in the hallway above.

"He's coming," she whispered, and grabbed Traci by the elbow and hustled her toward the back door.

"Hey," Traci cried, juggling her sopaipilla to keep from dropping it. "Who said I was leaving? I want to meet your mystery zillionaire guest."

Ali opened the back door. "He's not my zillionaire, and you can't meet him."

"Why not?"

She gave Traci a nudge over the threshold. "I already told you. He doesn't want anyone to know he's here." Before Traci could demand to stay, she shut the door in her face and turned the lock, just in case she tried sneaking back in.

With Traci dealt with, she headed for the breakfast room where she found Garrett standing at the buffet, pouring himself a cup of coffee. He was dressed much as he had been the day before—jeans and a black pullover sweater, a casual look she found extremely sexy.

Too bad his personality kills his appeal, she thought with regret.

Forcing a smile, she crossed to greet him. "Good morning. Did you sleep well?"

He spared her a glance, before returning the carafe to the hot plate. "Not particularly."

She kept her smile in place, refusing to let his sour disposition infect her. "Well, hopefully you'll rest better tonight."

He raised the cup to his lips and met her gaze over its rim. "That remains to be seen."

Those eyes again, she thought. What was it about them that was so mesmerizing? It certainly wasn't their color. Brown eyes were as common as house flies in Texas. So why were his so compelling?

Feeling herself being drawn deeper and deeper into their dark depths, she tore her gaze away and made a beeline for the kitchen.

"Have a seat at the table," she called over her shoulder. "I'll be right back with your breakfast."

Once out of his sight, she grabbed a plate and gave herself a stern lecture, as she filled it with food. He's nothing special, she told herself. Good-looking men were a dime a dozen in Austin. And so what if he was rich as sin? She'd never considered money a positive attribute, especially in a man. All the rich guys she'd ever known were pompous jackasses, who used their money to feed their egos and need for power. Cars, boats, homes. The more attention a "thing" drew to him, the greater its appeal.

Nope, she mentally confirmed, as she pulled the basket of sopaipillas from the oven. Garrett Miller was nothing special and definitely not a man she'd want to become involved with.

Adding the basket to the tray, she returned to the breakfast room, feeling much more in control.

"I hope you're hungry," she said, as she transferred dishes from the tray. "Huevos Rancheros," she said, identifying each food item as she arranged it in front of him. "Roasted new potatoes, fresh fruit with a light poppyseed dressing and sopaipillas with butter and honey."

Tucking the tray beneath her arm, she reached for the carafe. "If you need anything," she said after topping off his coffee, "I'll be in the kitchen."

She waited until the swinging door closed behind her, then set aside the tray and headed straight for the sink, anxious to put the kitchen back in order. Elbow deep in suds, washing the pans she'd dirtied while cooking, she heard the door open behind her and glanced over her shoulder. Her eyes shot wide when she saw Garrett entering, carrying his plate and cup of coffee.

"Is something wrong with the food?" she asked in alarm.

"No. I thought I'd eat in here with you."

She blinked in surprise. "But—but guests don't

eat in the kitchen. They take their meals in the breakfast room."

He set his cup and plate on the island and slid onto a stool. "This one doesn't," he said, and opened his napkin over his lap.

She considered insisting he return to the breakfast room, then turned back to the sink with a sigh, deciding the guy had paid for the right to eat wherever he wanted.

Thinking she should try to make conversation with him, she asked, "Do you have plans for the day?"

"Nothing specific. I thought I'd take a drive later and familiarize myself with the city."

"Have you ever been to Austin before?"

"A couple of times on business, but I was in meetings and saw very little of the city."

She rinsed the soap from the pan she'd washed and set it on the drainboard. "That's a shame. There's a lot to do and see in Austin."

"Such as…?"

She wrung out the dishcloth and moved to the island to wipe down the surface. "Well, there's Sixth Street," she said, "which is a little bit like Bourbon Street in New Orleans' French Quarter. You'll find everything there from tattoo parlors to jazz clubs. It gets pretty crazy on weekends. Lots of people on the street, drinking and partying.

"The State Capitol is a must-see," she went on. "Fabulous architecture and a tremendous view of the city from the top. And if you're into history, Austin is the home of the Lyndon Baines Johnson Library, as well as the Bob Bullock Museum."

"Have you lived here all your life?" he asked.

She chuckled, amused that he would mistake her for a native. "No. I'd think my northern accent would give me away."

"Northern?" he repeated, then shook his head and speared a plump strawberry with his fork. "Trust me. Whatever accent you had was lost to a Texas twang long ago."

"Really?" she said, considering that the ultimate compliment.

"Really. Throw in a couple more y'alls and you could pass for Sue Ellen from the *Dallas* TV series."

"Wow. That really takes me back. I watched that show when I was a kid. Sue Ellen, J.R., Bobby...." Hiding a smile, she shook her head. "The Ewing family was so dysfunctional, they made mine look like the Waltons." Reaching the end of the island where the coffeemaker sat, she lifted the carafe. "More coffee?"

"None for me." He wiped his mouth with his napkin, then set it beside his plate. "You've mentioned your family several times and not necessarily in a good light."

She shrugged. "Just being honest. My parents are strange people." She carried the carafe to the sink. "If you have any food preferences," she said, changing the subject, "let me know. I try to accommodate my guests' tastes whenever I can."

When he didn't reply, she glanced over her shoulder and found him frowning at her back. "Is something wrong?"

He shook his head. "No. I...I was just wondering if you'd have time to drive me around today."

Her stomach clenched at the thought of being trapped in a car with him all day. "If you're worried about getting lost, I can provide you with plenty of maps."

"I don't need a map. It's your opinion I want, as well as your knowledge of the area. You seem to know the city well and can probably offer me insight on things I wouldn't think to ask."

"I don't know," she said slowly, while trying to think of a plausible excuse to refuse him. "I've got a lot to do today. I finished boxing up all the Christmas decorations yesterday, but I still need to carry all the crates to the attic."

"Tell you what," he said. "If you'll act as my tour guide for the day, I'll help you haul the crates upstairs. And," he added, as if sensing her reluctance, "I'll compensate you for your time."

"You'll pay me?" she said in surprise.

"Yes."

He named an amount that made her jaw drop. "That's more than some people pay for a car!"

"I assure you I can afford it." He lifted a brow. "So? Do we have a deal?"

"Well, yeah," she said, then stuck out a hand, fearing he'd try to renege on the deal later. "In Texas, a man's handshake is as good as his word."

He took her hand. "Is it the same for a woman?"

The tingle started in the center of her palm and worked its way up her arm. Wondering what it was about him that spawned the sensation, she curled her fingers into a fist against her palm.

"Yeah," she said, surprised by the breathy quality in her voice. "Same goes."

If the computer industry ever bottomed-out and Garrett suddenly found himself in need of a job, he thought he might try his luck as a private investigator. He was getting pretty damn good at this clandestine stuff. Asking Ali to chauffeur him around Austin might have been spontaneous, but it was pure genius. Not only had he finessed a large block of time in which to learn more about her, he'd also finagled a way to check out her attic. He hadn't expected to find the missing deed lying in plain sight up there—and he hadn't—but he had familiarized himself with the attic's layout, which would come in handy if Ali refused to relinquish her portion of the deed to him, and he was forced to search for it on his own.

He hoped it didn't come to that. Lying was one thing. Stealing was quite another.

"Am I driving too fast?"

He glanced Ali's way. "No. Why?"

"You were frowning."

"Was I?" He turned his gaze to the roadway again. "Just thinking."

"You must think all the time."

"What makes you say that?"

"Because you're always frowning."

"Am I?" He considered the possibility a moment, then shrugged again. "I've never noticed."

"Do you ever have happy thoughts? Things that would make you smile?"

"Like what?"

"I don't know. A pleasant memory. Maybe a funny movie you've seen that makes you laugh when you think about it."

"I don't recall the last comedy I saw."

She glanced his way. "Are you serious?"

"Why would I lie?"

Shaking her head, she turned her gaze back to the road. "So what do you do for grins?"

"I enjoy playing computer games."

She spun a finger in the air. "Whoopee."

"What do *you* do for fun?" he asked, neatly turning the tables on her.

"There's very little I do that's *not* fun. Going out

to dinner or to the movies with friends. Working in my garden. Taking pictures."

"Taking pictures doesn't count. That's a job."

"Just because it's a job doesn't mean it can't be fun."

Realizing that she had unwittingly offered him the opportunity to probe into her life for that weakness he needed, he decided to take advantage of it. "If you enjoy photography so much, why have the bed-and-breakfast? Why not be a full-time photographer?"

"At one time, that was my plan. I was going to travel the world, taking pictures, then publish them as books."

"An album of your personal travels?" he said, as if doubting there was a market for such a thing.

"It wouldn't be personal," she told him. "At least, not in the way you mean. The pictures would be of people, places and things that share a theme or tell a particular story."

"What do you mean, 'tell a story'?"

"Well, let's say I wanted to do a photographic study of an Amish family," she said. "I'd photograph them at work, at play, in their home, in their community, capturing their lives, as well as their lifestyle on film. The pictures would tell the story."

"Isn't that the same as theme?"

"In some ways, yes. But when I think of theme, I think in terms of a single topic. Take poverty for instance," she said. "If I were to choose that as my theme, I might travel around, photographing examples of poverty in different parts of the country or even the world. Poverty would be obvious in all the pictures, but the people and the settings would be different."

That she enjoyed photography was obvious in the enthusiasm in her voice, the light in her eyes. "And if you chose families as a theme, you'd photograph different families, not just one."

"Score!" she cried and held up a hand to give him a high five.

Amused, he slapped her hand. "As interesting as all that is, it doesn't explain why you're running a bed-and-breakfast and not focusing on photography."

"Long and depressing story," she said, and slanted him a look. "Sure you want to hear it?"

He opened his hands. "I asked, didn't I?"

"Oh, wait," she said, straining to look at something up ahead. "There's Callahan's. Do you mind if we stop?"

"What's Callahan's?"

"A store. I need to pick up a bag of birdseed for my feeders."

Though disappointed that the stop would interrupt what he hoped would be an enlightening view into her life, he shrugged, thinking he'd pick up on the conversation again later. "Fine with me."

"Thanks. It'll save me making a trip later." She checked the rearview mirror for traffic, then changed lanes and turned into the parking lot. After shutting off the engine, she reached over the back seat for her tote. "Do you want to come in?"

He looked at the storefront, considering, then figured what the hell. There didn't appear to be many customers. "I believe I do."

As they entered the store, Ali nudged his arm. "Aren't you going to take off your sunglasses?" she whispered.

He shook his head. "Someone might recognize me."

With a roll of her eyes, she went in search of her birdseed. He watched her walk away and his gaze slid unerringly to the sway of her hips. Yeah, she was stacked, all right, he confirmed. He watched until she disappeared from sight, enjoying the view, then turned down an aisle to explore the store's merchandise on his own.

The place reminded him of the general stores he'd seen in Western movies, carrying everything from horse tack to Western-style clothing. He paused beside a display of cowboy hats and, curious, plucked a black one from the rack. He snugged it over his head and leaned to check out his reflection in the mirror behind the counter.

"Looks good."

He glanced over and saw Ali had joined him. Feeling foolish, he dragged off the hat. "I don't wear hats."

"Really? You should. Especially a cowboy hat. You look sexy in one."

He gave her a doubtful look.

"Well, you do," she insisted. "Sort of like a bad-ass gunslinger. You know. The kind who can empty a saloon by simply walking in the door."

Hiding a smile, he ran a finger along the brim. "Maybe I should buy it and wear it to my next board meeting."

"Couldn't hurt." She took the hat from him and placed it on his head again. She studied him a moment, and he'd swear he heard wheels begin to churn in her head.

"Come on," she said and grabbed his hand. "If you're going for the gunslinger look, you're gonna need jeans and boots."

He hung back. "I was kidding."

She gave him an impatient tug. "I wasn't. Besides, you know what they say. When in Rome…"

Garrett discovered the woman was a whirlwind when on a mission. Within minutes, she had him in a dressing room, trying on jeans, shirts, boots and what she referred to as a "duster," which was nothing more than a long trench coat with a Western-style yoke and a slit up the back so that a man could sit in a saddle while wearing it.

"Aren't you dressed *yet?*" she called impatiently from the other side of the door.

He hooked the silver belt buckle at his waist, then glanced up at his reflection in the mirror. He did a double take, startled by the change the style of clothing made to his appearance. "Yeah," he said staring. "I'm dressed."

"Well, come on out. I want to see."

He plucked the black felt hat from the hook on the wall and snugged it over his head as he stepped out of the dressing room.

A flash went off, and he caught himself just short of diving for cover.

Ali slowly lowered her digital camera to stare. "Wow," she murmured. "You don't even look like the same guy."

He scowled, embarrassed that, for a split second, he'd mistaken the flash of the camera for a gunshot.

"If I didn't know better," she went on, "I'd never guess you were Garrett Miller, zillionaire entrepreneur."

"Zillionaire?" Shaking his head, he turned to study himself in the full-length mirror. "You know," he said, growing thoughtful. "This getup might be just what I need to keep from being recognized."

"Like I said," Ali said, with a shrug, "when in Rome…" She reached to tear the price tag off his shirt.

He yanked his arm back. "What are you doing?"

She spun him around to rip the tag off the rear pocket of the jeans. "Taking off the price tags. Don't worry," she assured him as she gathered from the dressing room the clothes he'd worn into the store, as well as the stack of clothing he hadn't tried on yet, "I'll give them to the salesclerk, along with these other clothes. That way you can wear your new duds out of the store and not have to change again."

Ali held the camera before her face with one hand, and directed Garrett with the other. "A little to the left. A little more. Stop! Perfect." She clicked off a half-dozen or more shots, then dropped the camera to swing from her neck. "Now let's try a few with you standing with one boot propped on the boulder."

He dropped his hands to his hips in frustration. "I'm not a damn model, you know."

"No," she said patiently. "And I'm not a chauffeur, yet I've been driving you around all day like I was."

"A duty you're being well paid for," he reminded her.

She wrinkled her nose. "Oh, yeah. Right. Tell you what," she said. "Pose for a few more shots, and I'll give you a full set of prints, no charge."

"'A few shots' is all I agreed to when you talked me into this nonsense more than an hour ago."

"Can I help it if you're such a handsome model?"

"Flattery will get you nowhere," he said dryly.

"Okay. How about this? You let me take a few more pictures, and I'll chauffeur you around the whole month you're in town."

He frowned a moment, as if considering, then nodded. "All right. You've got yourself a deal."

Grinning, she drew the camera before her face again. "Boot on the boulder," she instructed. "Forearm braced on the knee. Now look off into the distance and make that face you make when you're thinking really hard. Great!" she exclaimed, and clicked away. "Man, you should see this. The sun is setting just behind your left shoulder and creating perfect shadows on your face.

"Give me a forlorn look," she said, continuing to click off shots. "You know. Like you've been running from the law for months, and you're missing that pretty little saloon girl you met up in Dodge City."

"A saloon girl in Dodge City?" He dropped his head back and laughed. "Damn, Ali, where do you get this stuff?"

The transformation laughter made to his face almost made her drop her camera, but she managed to hold on to it and keep clicking. "Part of the job," she told him. "Just part of the job."

Shaking his head, he dragged his foot from the boulder. "You should be a writer, not a photographer." When he realized she was still taking pictures, he held up a hand to block her view. "Would you stop," he complained. "You must've taken a hundred pictures or more."

She reluctantly lowered the camera. "I'll be lucky if a third are worth anything."

He went stock-still. "You didn't say anything about selling these pictures."

"Would you lighten up?" she said, laughing. "I took the pictures for fun, not to sell. Kind of a souvenir for you of your trip to Texas."

"Oh," he said in relief. "Which reminds me," he said, and plopped down on the boulder, stretched out his legs. "You were going to tell me why you're running a bed-and-breakfast, rather than focusing on a career in photography."

Gathering up her tote, she crossed to sit beside him. "Are you sure you want to hear this?" she asked, as she pulled her camera over her head. "It's really boring."

"I wouldn't have asked, if I didn't."

With a shrug, she tucked the camera into her tote. "It goes back to when I dropped out of college during my junior year and moved to Austin."

"Why did you drop out?"

"My parents come from a long line of doctors and they expected me to follow in their footsteps. Carry on the family tradition. That kind of thing."

"And you didn't want to?"

"Not even a little. I did try," she said in her defense. "But I hated all the science courses I was required to take and my grades proved it. I tried to talk my parents into letting me change my major, but they wouldn't listen. They kept saying I wasn't applying myself. That being a doctor was an honorable occupation, a duty even. We argued about it all during Christmas break, and I finally told them that they couldn't force me to become a doctor, that I was going to sign up for the courses *I* wanted to take."

"And did you?"

She grimaced. "For all the good it did me. When they received the bill from the university for my spring tuition and saw what courses I'd signed up for, they refused to pay it. When that didn't whip me into line, they closed the checking account they'd set up for me to pay my college expenses, which left me with no money and no way to pay for my housing, food. Nothing."

"So how did you end up in Texas?"

"Claire Fleming. She and I met our freshman year in college and became best friends. She knew my parents had cut me off and how bummed I was. To cheer me up, she invited me to go to Austin with her to visit her grandmother. I had nothing better to do, so I tagged along.

"To make a long story a little shorter, the Vista belongs to Claire's grandmother, Margaret Fleming. It was a wedding present from her first husband. Sadly he died after they'd been married only a few years. She remarried several years later to some oil guy and moved to Saudi Arabia, but she held on to the house. Said selling it would be like cutting out her heart.

"She came back to the States several times a year

for month-long visits and always stayed at the house. As she got older, it became harder for her to travel and she wasn't able to come as often. You can imagine what happened to the house. What the vandals didn't destroy, varmints did. It was a mess. She'd always hoped that Claire would want the house someday, but Claire fell in love with an Aussie and was planning to move to Australia right after graduation, which she did, by the way. So the grandmother decided to make one final trip to Austin before selling the house. Claire was to meet her there and help her pack up what personal belongings she wanted to keep.

"What I didn't know was that Claire and her grandmother had already discussed my situation, and they'd decided to offer the house to me." She held up a hand. "And, yes, I know it sounds too good to be true. At the time, I thought so, too. But Mimi—that's Claire's grandmother—was dead serious. She really loved the house and didn't want to sell it, and she definitely didn't need the money. So she offered it to me. All she asked in return was that I take care of it and love it as much as she did."

"Sounds like the perfect arrangement."

"It was a sweet deal, all right, but it only resolved my need for housing. I was still broke and without a job. Mimi, Claire and I brainstormed ways I could earn money to cover my expenses and still have time to go to school, and we came up with the idea of renting out the extra bedrooms to college students. It was the perfect setup for me. Since the house is on Town Lake and relatively close to the university, I never had a problem leasing the rooms, which meant I could be really selective about who I leased to."

"If it was such a success, why the change to a bed-and-breakfast?"

She lifted a brow and looked down her nose at him. "Have you ever lived with twelve college students?" She shuddered, remembering. "It was bedlam even on the best day. And there was absolutely no privacy. After I graduated, I decided I wanted the house to be more like a home than a dorm, and I came up with the idea of turning the Vista into a bed-and-breakfast."

"And the grandmother was okay with the change?"

"More than okay. In fact, she gave me the house."

"*Gave* it to you?" he repeated.

She nodded. "I think she'd reconciled herself to the fact that Claire was never going to want it, and she definitely didn't want her son to get his hands on it, so she decided to give it to me."

"Gave it to you," he repeated, doubting her story, since his research had indicated the only property Ali owned was her car.

"It's not official yet," she was quick to tell him. "She only told me about her decision last summer, then she caught pneumonia and passed away just before Thanksgiving. Her estate was sizable, to say the least, so it'll probably take a while for her lawyers to get everything prepared for probate and the necessary papers filed to transfer ownership to me."

She glanced around, and was surprised to see it was getting dark. She hitched the strap to her tote over her shoulder. "I had no idea it was getting so late. We'd better go."

He stood, and offered her a hand.

When she grasped his hand, she felt that now familiar spark of electricity between their palms and watched his face as he pulled her to her feet, wondering if he felt it, too.

"Did you feel that?" she asked.

"What?"

"That sparkly thing when our hands touched."

"Sparkly thing?" He shook his head. "No, can't say that I did."

"Really?" she said in surprise, then frowned and rubbed thoughtfully at her palm. "That's weird. I feel it every time we touch."

Three

Sparkly thing?

Garrett snorted as he climbed into bed. How about a hundred volts of electricity shooting up his arm?

But he sure as hell wasn't going to admit that to Ali. If he'd learned nothing else during his thirty-six years of living, it was never reveal your weaknesses to your enemy.

Enemy?

Frowning thoughtfully, he folded his hands behind his head, and stared up at the ceiling, unsure if that tag still fit. If the stories Ali had told him today were true, she was looking more like a victim, than the enemy.

Her dropping out of college up north and finishing her education in Texas was true enough. He'd un-earthed that nugget about her past while doing his own research prior to making the trip to Austin. But nothing he'd found had indicated her move to Texas was due to her parents cutting her off. He might've dismissed her story as exaggeration, if he hadn't already heard his stepmother describe her adoptive parents as cold and heartless people. But in Garrett's opinion, what Ali's parents had done to her was inexcusable. Imagine, a parent who would knowingly leave his child with no money, no job and no prospects…

He shook his head ruefully. Ali was just damn lucky she'd had a fairy godmother waiting in the wings. No telling what would've happened to her if Mimi and Claire hadn't come along, offering her a place to live, as well as the means to support herself.

He frowned, more than a little surprised by the level of compassion he felt building toward Ali. He was going to have to be careful, he told himself. Prior to coming to Austin, he'd had a laundry list of reasons to despise her. He couldn't allow a hard-luck story blind him to the hurt she'd caused his stepmother or allow it to distract him from his purpose for being in her home.

Her life might resemble Cinderella's, but he sure as hell was no Prince Charming, prepared to charge onto the scene to rescue her.

If anything, he'd come to destroy her.

To prove it, he reached for his cell phone and punched in the number of his lawyer.

"Hey, Tom. Garrett. Sorry to call you at home and at such a late hour, but I need you to do some research for me. See if you can locate information on a woman by the name of Margaret Fleming. Her last address was in Saudi Arabia, but she owned property in Austin, Texas.

"No," he replied to Tom's question. "This doesn't have anything to do with Future Concepts' expansion. This is…personal. The woman passed away last November. I want to know who inherited the house she owns in Austin."

He visited a moment longer, then disconnected the call and settled back on the bed.

Ali may not have realized it, he thought in satisfaction, but there was a strong possibility she'd given him the "price" he needed to win her cooperation. That she loved the house was obvious, and Garrett would bet his controlling shares of stock in Future Concepts that she didn't own it.

But *he* would before the month was out.

After chauffeuring Garrett around for three days, Ali had decided two things about her current guest. He had more mood swings than a pregnant woman, and he was the most impatient man she'd ever met in her life.

Most people would just kick back and relax, while riding in a car. Not Garrett. God forbid the man waste a second of his precious time. At the moment, he had his BlackBerry in his hand and was checking his e-mail, a task he had conducted at least four times during the day. It was almost ten o'clock at night, for heaven's sake! Was his correspondence so important he had to check it even at night?

Noticing the brake lights coming on ahead of her, Ali slowed, adjusting her speed to the long line of cars in front of her.

"Uh-oh."

Garrett lifted his gaze from his BlackBerry. "Uh-oh, what? Why are you stopping?"

She tipped her head at the traffic in front of them. "Construction. I forgot the highway crew closes down all but one lane at night so they can work on the interstate when there is less traffic."

Scowling, he closed his BlackBerry and began to drum his fingers impatiently on the console.

After sitting for five minutes at a standstill, he swore. "Dammit! This is ridiculous. There's got to be an alternate route."

She shook her head. "There's not. And even if there was," she added as she looked in the rearview mirror at the long stream of headlights behind her, "there's no way we can get off the interstate now. We're trapped between exits."

His scowl deepened.

The headlights on the cars ahead of her began to blink off, an indication that the drivers had resigned themselves to the delay and had turned off their engines. Ali followed suit, but left the radio playing.

He whipped his head around to peer at her. "Why did you turn off the car?"

She lifted a shoulder and slid down in her seat, making herself more comfortable. "No sense wasting gas. These delays can last up to a half hour or more."

"A half hour!"

"Would you lighten up?" she said with a laugh. "A little delay isn't going to kill you."

He burned her with a look, then turned his gaze back to the windshield to glare through the darkness at the stalled traffic.

Deciding he needed a distraction, she twisted the dial to an oldies' station and cranked up the radio to an earsplitting level.

He clapped his hands over his ears. "What the hell are you doing?" he cried.

She opened her door. "Creating a diversion," she replied as she climbed out. Rounding the hood, she opened the passenger door and grabbed his hand. "Come on, Garrett. They're playing our song."

"What?" he said in confusion, as she all but dragged him out of the car.

"Music. Dance. Get it?" She dropped her hands

to her hips, with a disgusted huff. "Don't tell me you don't know how to dance."

"I know how."

She placed a hand on his shoulder and stepped in close. "So dance with me."

Garrett shot an uneasy glance around at the cars behind them, sure that everyone was staring at them and laughing. "This is ridiculous," he muttered.

"No," she informed him. "It's spontaneous. Fun. Something I don't think you have nearly enough of."

He probably could've resisted, was sure he would have climbed back into the car, if she hadn't pressed her body against his and begun to sway to the slow beat of the Righteous Brothers' song pumping from the car's speakers.

Without conscious thought, he began to sway, too, his body moving in rhythm with hers. A heartbeat later he was guiding her in a slow dance around the car. Later he would be grateful for the darkness, the lack of headlights, would probably curse himself for the chance he had taken in exposing himself to the public eye and the danger he might well have put himself in. But at the moment, all he could think about was how perfectly her body melded to his, how naturally they moved together, how utterly *free* he felt dancing in the middle of an interstate highway with hundreds of people looking on.

The song ended and he swayed slowly to a stop. Instead of releasing her, he turned his face against her hair, painfully aware of every point where their bodies touched. He felt the quickening of her breath against his neck, the tremble of her fingers within his. One smooth glide of his lips over her hair and his mouth was on hers. The pleasure, the taste of her was like taking a fist in the gut, totally unexpected and hitting low and hard.

Her lips were pillows of satin beneath his, her taste an aphrodisiac that streamed through his bloodstream like fire. A part of him knew he should stop, that kissing her was a mistake, that he was chancing blowing the mission he'd come to Austin to accomplish. But he couldn't stop. It took the impatient sound of a car horn to force his mouth from hers. Even then he didn't release her. With his eyes on hers, he searched her gaze, found the same heat in them that fired his veins.

It was Ali who made the first move, taking a step back and hugging her jacket more closely around her. "Uh. Looks like traffic's starting to move."

He glanced toward the cars lined in front of them and saw that headlights were blinking on, engines were starting. "Yeah," he said dully, wondering what had come over him. "Let's get out of here."

Ali didn't know what had happened to Garrett overnight to put him in such a grumpy mood, but if it was because of the kiss they'd shared on the interstate, he could darn well get over it.

She just hoped she could.

She slid a glance his way. Who'd have thought he could kiss like that? Not her, that was for darn sure. In the blink of an eye, he'd turned a spontaneous street dance into a lustfest…and with very little effort on his part.

And she'd thought the tingles she'd felt when they touched were something. Ha! They were nothing compared to the kick she'd received when his lips had touched hers. She released a slow breath, the reminder alone enough to make her want to whip the car over to the shoulder and jump him.

She slanted him another look. So why wasn't he similarly affected? From the moment he'd appeared for breakfast, he'd done nothing but scowl. And as for conversation… Well, there wasn't any. They'd been driving all morning, with him giving two-word commands—turn right, turn left, leaving her with no sense of where he wanted to go or exactly what he was looking for.

And as far as the kiss went… Well, he hadn't said a word about *that*.

She firmed her lips. Well, if that's the way he wanted to play it, she could pretend it hadn't happened, too.

"Maybe if you told me what kind of property you're interested in," she said, "I could be of more help."

He continued to frown at the map displayed on the screen of his portable GPS. "A minimum of ten acres, preferably more."

"What about accessibility to public transportation?" she asked, hoping to narrow the parameters somewhat. "Wouldn't that factor into where you'd want to build?"

"Not necessarily."

"Great," she muttered under her breath. "Another irresponsible employer adding to Austin's already burgeoning traffic problems."

He glanced her way. "I'm not irresponsible."

"If you build where there's no access to public transportation, you are," she informed him. "You'd be adding to traffic and that's irresponsible in my book."

Scowling, he turned off the GPS. "For your information, I consider the effect my company has on a city's traffic, as well as its effect on the environment."

"How?" she challenged, doubting that he considered anything but profits when he made decisions regarding his company.

"At the current facilities on the East Coast, we offer a shuttle service from specified locations around the city. Employees who take advantage of the shuttle, and those who ride in a carpool with a minimum of two other employees, receive monetary rewards for their efforts. If I build a complex in Austin, I'll implement the same policy here."

"If?" she repeated. "I thought building here was a foregone conclusion."

"Only if I'm able to find a suitable site."

"Oh."

"Yeah. Oh."

Having had enough of his sour disposition, she tightened her hands on the wheel. "Why are you in such a bad mood?"

He set the GPS on the floorboard at his feet. "I'm not in a bad mood."

"Well, you darn sure look like you are." She held up a hand. "Oh, wait. I forget that expression is normal for you."

He nailed her with a look. "Are you purposely trying to tick me off? If so, you're doing a damn good job."

That's it, she thought angrily and whipped the car to the side of the road. She'd had all she was going to take of his sour attitude. Ramming the gearshift into Park, she spun on the seat to face him. "Don't try blaming your bad mood on me," she warned. "You were grumpy when we started out this morning."

"Well, maybe if I could get a good night's sleep, I'd be in a better mood," he shot back at her.

"And you're not sleeping is my fault?"

"It is if you're the one responsible for putting that lousy mattress on the bed."

Her jaw dropped. "There's nothing wrong with that mattress! It's top-of-the-line and almost new."

"It sags on one side."

"So sleep on the other! Better yet, sleep in a different bed. You leased the entire house. Pick another one to sleep in."

"Fine. I want yours."

She gaped. "You *what?*"

"I want yours. You said I could have my pick."

"I didn't mean mine!"

"Why not? You said I could have my pick."

"Of the rooms you *leased,*" she informed him.

"Too late. You already said I could have my pick, and I choose your bed."

She fought for patience. "If you want to sleep in one of the other rooms upstairs, fine. You certainly paid for the right to sleep wherever you want."

"I certainly did," he agreed, "and I choose to sleep in your bed."

She started to respond, then closed her mouth and narrowed her eyes in suspicion. "You're just trying to avoid the real issue, aren't you?"

"And that would be…?"

"Kissing me last night. Well, let me tell you something, buddy," she went on before he could say anything. "It was no big deal. Okay? As far as I'm concerned it's forgotten. Over. Done with. Never happened."

"Oh, really?"

"Yeah, really. I—"

Before she could finish, his mouth was on hers, smothering her words. There was no slow buildup to *this* kiss. His mouth came down hard on hers, forcing her head back against the seat and her pulse into a gallop. She tasted the anger in him, the heat. A split second later his lips softened, sweeping over hers with a seductive slowness that stole her breath, before he nipped at her lower lip and withdrew. She opened her eyes to find he'd settled in his seat again, his gaze on the windshield.

"Let's check out the area around Bastrop."

She stared, wondering if she'd imagined it all. "B-Bastrop?"

"Yeah. From the map I was looking at, it appears to be near Austin, yet far enough away that parcels of land are probably still sold by the acre, rather than by the square inch."

She straightened and pulled the gearshift into Drive, her hand shaking a bit. "B-Bastrop's a nice town," she said, anxious to prove she was as unaffected by the kiss as he seemed to be. "Lots of history and beautiful old homes. I would imagine their tax base is lower than Austin's, which would be a bonus for your company and whatever employees might choose to live there."

He pointed to a convenience store up ahead. "Pull over and I'll buy a paper, so we can check out what's for sale."

She turned into the parking lot and pulled up alongside the newspaper rack, her pulse rate almost back to normal. "Wouldn't it be easier to just call a Realtor?"

"It would," he agreed, as he climbed from the car, then ducked his head back inside. "Better yet, why don't I just rent a billboard and announce to the whole world I'm here looking for land?" Muttering under his breath, he slammed the door and strode for the newspaper stand.

Jerk, she thought resentfully as she watched him feed coins into the slot. His paranoia about keeping his presence in Austin a secret was wearing thin. She could see how it made good business-sense for him to play his cards close to his chest. But wasn't he carrying this a little far? He never took a step out of the house without those stupid sunglasses. And earlier, when she stopped at the window of a fast-food joint to order sodas, he'd slumped down in the seat and kept his face averted, like he was afraid someone was going to recognize him, which was totally nuts. It wasn't like he was a movie star or something. He was a business-man, for cripes' sake! Prior to him coming to the Vista, if she had passed him on the street, she wouldn't have even given him a second look.

Unfortunately he chose that moment to bend over to pull a newspaper from the rack, giving her a full view of his nicely shaped butt, and her mouth went dry as dust. Okay, she admitted, wetting her lips. Maybe she would've looked twice. But she doubted she would've

recognized him. And even if she had, it wouldn't have occurred to her that he was in Austin to buy property. For all she'd know, he could be on vacation. All this hush-hush, top-secret stuff was ridiculous.

He jumped into the car and slid down in the seat as he slammed the door. "Drive!"

She blinked in surprise. "Excuse me?"

He lifted his head slightly to peer out the rear window, then dropped back down. "I think the guy at the gas pump recognized me."

"So?"

"So get the hell out of here!" he shouted.

She stomped on the accelerator and careened onto the highway, sending the rearend of the car fishtailing crazily.

"Is he following us?" he asked.

She looked in the rearview mirror and saw that the truck had indeed pulled onto the highway behind them. "I don't know that he's following us, but he is behind us."

"Speed up."

Though she wasn't sure the rental she was driving could outrun the truck, she pressed down harder on the accelerator.

"Is he still there?" he asked after a minute.

She glanced in the rearview mirror again. "Yeah. About four car-lengths behind."

"Faster."

She shot him a look. "Are you crazy? I'm already going thirty over the speed limit."

"So go fifty! Just lose him."

She glanced in the rearview mirror again. "Uh-oh," she murmured, and lifted her foot off the accelerator.

"What are you doing?" he yelled. "I said speed up, not slow down!"

"I don't know what whirling red lights mean where you're from," she told him, "but in Texas, they mean pull over."

He sat up and looked out the rear window. "Ah, hell," he groaned, then turned to scowl at her. "You might have told me the cops around here drive unmarked vehicles."

"And ruin your fun?" she said sweetly. She hit the button to lower the window and greeted the patrolman approaching the car. "Good morning, Officer."

He touched a finger to the brim of his hat. "Morning, ma'am. Is there a reason you were driving forty-five miles per hour over the speed limit?"

"Only one," she replied, and hooked a thumb over her shoulder at Garrett. "Him."

Garrett hissed a breath between his teeth, then yanked off his sunglasses and leaned around Alito look up at the policeman. "My fault entirely," he said. "I didn't realize you were a police officer."

"Ah," the patrolman said, nodding. "So speeding's all right, so long as the law isn't around."

"No, no, no," Garrett replied in frustration. "That's not what I meant, at all. I was buying a newspaper and saw you watching me. I thought you'd recognized me, so I told Ali to lose you."

"Why don't you dig yourself a little deeper?" Ali said under her breath.

Garrett burned her with a look, then shifted his gaze to the police officer again. "I'm Garrett Miller," he said, as if that explained everything.

The officer looked at Ali. "What? Is he some kind of rock star or something?"

Ali rolled her lips inward, to keep from laughing. "Uh. No, sir. He owns Future Concepts, a computer company."

When the officer's expression remained blank, she looked over at Garrett and shrugged. "Your turn."

"It's not funny," Garrett snapped as he flopped down on the sofa.

"No, it's not," Ali agreed, trying her best to hide her smile. "But if you could have seen your face when Officer Wilhelm told you to put your hands on the trunk of the car and spread 'em…." She sputtered a laugh, unable to help herself. "Now *that* was funny!"

Scowling, he folded his arms across his chest. "Well, I'm glad you found it humorous. Being frisked like a common criminal certainly isn't my idea of fun."

"I'd think you'd be relieved," she said, feigning wide-eyed innocence. "You told him everything about yourself except your favorite color of underwear and he still didn't have a clue who you were."

"No, but the dispatcher recognized my name."

"Which is all that saved you from taking a ride in the backseat of a patrol car," she reminded him.

"You're really enjoying this, aren't you?"

She didn't even try to hide her smile. "Uh-huh."

"Why?"

"Honestly? Because I think you place way too much importance on yourself."

He lifted a brow. "Oh, really."

"Yes, really. You need to lighten up. Forget you're a zillionaire for a while. Kick up your heels and have some fun for a change."

He snorted. "You don't have a clue what it's like to be me."

"Other than boring, no."

"Boring?" He pushed to his feet, his jaw clenched in anger. "Let me tell you what it's like to be me," he said, bearing down on her. "Money attracts people, including crazies and crooks. And unlike our friendly police officer this morning, most people recognize my name, if not my face, which causes problems for me. Because of my success, I haven't been able to fly commercially in years. I can't go to a movie theater or a restaurant, or anywhere for that matter, without

drawing attention. If I do venture out to a highly pub-
licized event, I'm forced to take a bodyguard along,
just in case some lunatic decides to try to kidnap me
for ransom.

"And as for having fun," he continued, "unless it can
be boxed and delivered for me to enjoy in the privacy
of my home, I can forget it. Going out in public is a
freedom I lost the day I made my first million."

By the time he finished his tirade, he was standing
nose to nose with Ali, so close she could feel the
warmth of his breath on her mouth.

"I—I had no idea," she stammered.

"Most people don't. They envy my success, even
try to emulate it, but they don't know what success
has cost me, what it would cost them if it was theirs."
Hiding a smile, he turned away. "But you'll get a
taste of it soon enough."

She tensed. "What do you mean?"

"Our good friend Officer Wilhelm gave us his
word he wouldn't tell anyone about seeing me, but
I'll bet you money he tells someone. Or the dispatcher will. And if one of them does tell, you can
expect the media to start arriving by morning."

Her eyes rounded. "Here?"

"Here and anywhere we dare venture. Media
hounds are like fleas on a dog. Irritating as hell and
all but impossible to get rid of."

* * *

Ali paced the living room, stealing an occasional peek through the blinds she'd closed. So far, so good, she thought. Not a person or a car in sight.

Confident that Officer Wilhelm had been true to his word—or Garrett had exaggerated his own importance, which is what she felt was more the case—she abandoned her watch and went to the kitchen for something to drink.

"I'm getting a glass of wine," she called to him in the den. "Do you want one?"

"Yes, please."

She filled two glasses and carried them to the den. She glanced over her shoulder at the television as she handed Garrett his drink. "What are you watching?"

"Jeopardy."

Figures, she thought, biting back a smile, as she sank down on the sofa beside him. "Who's winning?" she asked.

"Guy on the left. They're about to start Double Jeopardy, though, so that could change things."

A commercial came on and he lifted the remote to surf through channels.

"Do you have something against commercials?" she asked in frustration.

"Other than being an utter waste of my time?" He shook his head. "Not particularly."

"You advertise," she reminded him.

"Some."

"Hypocrite."

"Why? Because I refuse to watch a boring commercial?"

She opened a hand. "If the shoe fits…"

"It's marketing's responsibility to capture the attention of the consumer. If they fail—" he clicked the remote "—which my company's commercials seldom do," he informed her, "I change channels until I find something that does catch my attention. Like that," he said and set the remote aside.

"The stock market report?" She fanned her face. "Stop. Please. I'm not sure my heart can take the excitement."

He shot her a scowl. "Why don't you go spy on the reporters lurking outside some more?"

She tucked her feet beneath her and took a sip of her wine. "There's nobody out there."

"There will be by morning."

"You're full of bologna. No reporters are coming here."

"Wanna bet?"

"As a matter of fact, I do," she said.

"Five hundred says they'll be here by morning."

She considered, then shook her head. "Too rich for my blood."

"Okay, if you don't want to gamble cash, put up some of your photography of equal value."

She hesitated a moment, then stood and stuck out her hand. "All right, you've got yourself a deal."

He took her hand, but instead of shaking it, he used it to haul himself to his feet. "I prefer photos of landscape, rather than people."

She lifted a brow. "Kind of confident you're going to win, aren't you?"

He shot her a wink and turned away. "When it's a sure thing, I can afford to be."

She frowned at his back. "Where are you going?"

"To bed."

"Hey, wait a minute!" she cried, hurrying after him. "That's the way to my room."

"I know. Remember? I chose your bed to sleep in tonight."

"You're not sleeping in my bed!"

He opened the door to her private quarters. "Yes, I am."

She ran after him, praying she hadn't left underwear or any other equally embarrassing items lying around. "Garrett, really," she pleaded. "You can sleep in any bed you want. Just not mine."

He sank down on the side of her bed and bounced a couple of times, as if testing the mattress. "I prefer this one," he said, and stood, pulling his sweater over his head.

Ali stared, unable to tear her gaze away from the oh-so-sexy chest he'd exposed. Who'd've thought?

she thought, as heat crawled up her neck, threatening her air. She'd been pressed against his chest the night before when they'd kissed, but they had both had on jackets, which had done a heck of a job of concealing what proved to be a wonderfully muscled and toned body.

"You win," she managed to say, and darted for the adjoining bath. "Just let me get my stuff."

She grabbed her pajamas and toothbrush and hustled back out, careful to keep her gaze fixed straight ahead, fearing he'd stripped completely while she was out of the room. In the doorway, she groped blindly behind her for the knob, to pull the door closed behind her.

"Ali?"

She stopped, but didn't dare turn around. "What?"

"Since you enjoyed kissing me so much, I thought you'd want to sleep with me, too."

Setting her jaw, she slapped a hand against the wall switch, turning off the light, and yanked the door closed behind her.

She wasn't sure, but she'd swear she heard him laughing as she stalked to the den.

Score one for the home team, Garrett thought, chuckling, as he climbed into bed. Judging by Ali's fast exit following his comment about her sleeping with him, it appeared he'd succeeded in getting even with her for the hard time she'd given him over his run-in with the law and Officer Wilhelm.

He punched up his pillow and lay back, wondering where she would sleep. There were plenty of empty beds to choose from, including the one he'd slept in prior to claiming hers. He'd blamed his inability to sleep on the sagging mattress, which was what had started the whole where-will-Garrett-sleep debate. But Garrett's sleeplessness wasn't due to a sagging bed.

It was due to the Vista's innkeeper.

His smile faded. He hadn't intended for it to happen, had done everything within his power to prevent it, but it was true.

Ali Moran had gotten under his skin.

It had started with the stories she'd told him of her past and his growing suspicion that she was more victim than enemy, and had quickly escalated to a physical attraction that grew stronger each day he spent with her.

He dragged his pillow over his face to smother a groan. What the hell was he going to do now? he asked himself in frustration. He'd arrived in Austin prepared to despise her, ruin her if necessary, and now all he could think about was sleeping with her? She was his stepmother's daughter, for God's sake!

He could handle this, he told himself. It was simply a matter of refocusing his goals, keeping a respectable distance from her.

He drew in a deep breath, telling himself he could do this. He'd maintained his objectivity in tougher situations.

He was immediately proved wrong. That one breath had filled his senses with her scent, evoking images of her. Lying in this very bed. The two of them together. Her nude body wrapped around his like a vine.

Groaning, he rolled to his stomach and buried his face in the pillow.

"Focus," he told himself sternly. "Just focus on the damn goal."

He'd call his lawyer tomorrow, he promised himself. Find out if Tom had discovered who owned the Vista yet. Knowledge was power and power was what he needed to keep the scales weighted on his side…and hopefully his mind focused on his goal and not on the Vista's innkeeper.

Ali tiptoed into her bedroom and cautiously approached the bed. She really didn't want to wake Garrett—or be in the same room with him after the crack he'd made about her sleeping with him—but she preferred both to calling the police.

At the side of the bed, she leaned to touch his shoulder. The next thing she knew, she was flat on her back on the mattress and Garrett was straddling her, his fist reared back, like he was going to slug her.

"Garrett! It's me! Ali!"

He blinked, then rolled off her, swearing. "Dammit, Ali! Don't ever slip up on me like that again."

Eyeing him warily, she dragged herself up to a sitting position. "Don't worry. I won't."

He twisted around to switch on the bedside lamp, then slumped back against the headboard, scowling. "Sorry," he muttered, then glanced over at her. "I didn't hurt you, did I?"

"N-no. Scared me plenty, though." Realizing the skill and strength required to accomplish a move like the one he'd just performed, she asked, "Where'd you learn to do that?"

"Self-defense class." His scowl deepened. "When your life has been threatened as many times as mine, you take what precautions you can."

"Threatened?" she repeated.

"Yes, threatened." He slanted her a look. "Why were you sneaking around in my room, anyway?"

"I'd remind you it's *my* room, but we've got more pressing matters to worry about."

"Like what?"

"Like the men outside."

He shot up from the bed and ran to peer out the window.

The sight of him standing there in nothing but black silk boxer shorts was almost enough to make her forget about the men she'd seen skulking around outside.

Almost.

"You can't see them from there," she told him. "They're out front. On the street side of the rock wall."

He dove across the bed for the lamp and switched it off, plunging the room into darkness.

"What are you doing?" she cried.

He clapped a hand over her mouth. "Shh," he whispered. "We don't want them to know we're awake."

She shoved his hand away. "Why not?"

"If they think we're asleep and unaware of their presence, hopefully they'll stay where they are and wait for daylight before approaching the house."

"But I thought you didn't want them here?" she said in confusion.

"I don't." He dropped his elbows to his knees and his head to his hands. "We've got to think of a way to get out of here without them seeing us."

"*We?* As in you and me?" She shook her head. "Uh-uh. Sorry, buddy. But I'm not going anywhere with you."

"You have no choice."

"Oh, I have lots of choices," she informed him. "The most obvious is staying right here in my own house."

"You can't. It's no longer safe."

The somberness of his tone turned her blood to ice. "What do you mean, it's not safe? We're talking men toting cameras here, not Uzis."

"There's something I need to tell you," he said

hesitantly. "I wasn't completely honest with you about why I wanted my presence here kept a secret."

She dropped her head back with a moan. "I really hate middle of the night confessions."

"My life's been threatened."

She snapped her head back up to stare. "Somebody wants you dead?"

"It appears that way."

"But…why?"

"If I knew that, I'd probably know who wanted to kill me."

"And you think whoever that person is, is outside my house right now?"

"No. I'm fairly confident it's only photographers out there. But once they make my presence here known," he added, "I can almost promise you the person who threatened me will come here looking for me."

She stared, trying to make sense of what he was telling her, then held up a hand. "Wait a minute. Just because somebody wants you dead, doesn't mean I'm in danger."

"I'm afraid it does. If he comes here and finds me gone, he may take you."

"Me?" She choked a laugh. "Like anyone would want me," she said wryly.

"He would, if he thinks you're important to me."

Her heart faltered, then kicked hard against her chest. "You mean he might use me as a hostage?"

"It's possible and it's a chance I'm not willing to take."

Vivid images of every movie or news clip she'd seen involving hostages filled her mind. And not a one of them were pretty. "Oh my God," she whispered. "What are we going to do?"

"We're getting out of here." He rolled off the bed and snatched up his jeans, tugged them on. "I'm going upstairs to pack my stuff and make some phone calls. You'll need to pack a bag, too. Enough to hold you for a couple of weeks."

"A couple of weeks!" she cried. "I can't be gone a couple of weeks!"

"Hopefully you won't be," he told her. "And no lights," he warned, as he headed for the door. "We don't want them to suspect we're up to anything."

Garrett took the rear stairs two at a time and broke into a run when he reached the second floor. Getting out of Austin was imperative, but where to go was a problem. He couldn't call for his private jet. It would take too much time for his pilot to fly to Texas. Public transportation was out, as it made him too visible. That meant finding some place close to hide out for a while, somewhere no one would think to look for him.

He knew of only one place that fit his needs: his stepmother's son's ranch.

Muttering a curse, he paced his room. He didn't

want to call Jase. Calling him meant explaining where he was, what he was up to, and his stepmother had made them promise they wouldn't search for Ali, that they would respect her request for privacy and leave her alone.

But *he* hadn't promised, he reminded himself. Jase and Eddie, Jase's father, had promised.

Admonishing himself of any guilt for his actions, he pulled his cell phone from his briefcase and scrolled through the address book until he found Jase's home number.

Mandy, Jase's wife, answered on the second ring.

"Hello?" she said sleepily.

"Mandy, it's Garrett."

"Well, hey, Garrett," she said, sounding surprised to hear from him. "What are you doing calling me in the middle of the night?"

"I'm in a jam. Is Jase there?"

"He's in Washington visiting his mother. Haven't you seen him?"

"No, and I really need his help."

"Call him at Barbara's. I'm sure he'll do whatever he can to help you out."

"I can't call him at Barbara's," he said in frustration. "You'll have to help."

"You know I'll do whatever I can, but wouldn't it make better sense to just call Jase, since he's in Washington and I'm in Texas?"

"That's just it. I'm in Texas, too."

"What!" she cried. "Where?"

"Ali Moran's house."

A pregnant pause followed his announcement.

"You're at Ali's?" she said.

"Yes. I'll explain later, but we need a place to hide out for a couple of days. I was hoping we could stay in one of the hunting cabins."

"Of course you can," she told him, then asked hesitantly, "Does Ali know you're Barbara's stepson?"

"No, and you've got to promise me you'll keep it that way."

"Are you sure you know what you're doing?" she asked doubtfully. "Barbara made y'all promise you'd leave Ali alone."

He felt a stab of guilt and quickly shrugged it off. "Jase and Eddie promised. I promised nothing."

"That's splitting hairs, don't you think?"

He drew in a breath. "We can discuss this later, okay? Right now I've got to get us out of Austin."

"Okay. But when Barbara finds out about this, I'm pointing all ten fingers at you, buddy. Understand? I'm not chancing getting on my mother-in-law's bad side just to save your butt, even if it is a cute one."

The next call Garrett made was to the head of his company's security department.

"Joe, it's Garrett. We've got a problem."

Four

The plan Garrett devised for his and Ali's escape included every mode of transportation, with the exception of air. He probably would've considered that, too, if he or Ali had known how to fly.

Their adventure started on land, with them sneaking down to the pier and climbing aboard the rowboat Ali kept on hand for her guests to use. With moonlight as their only illumination, they'd rowed across the lake and docked near the shoreline of the Hyatt Regency. From there, they'd grabbed a taxi for the airport, where Garrett had insisted Ali rent a vehicle, claiming if he rented it he would be leaving a paper trail that could easily be followed.

After loading their luggage into the rental, they'd left Austin, with Ali behind the wheel. She had thought he would insist on driving, had even suggested it, but he had reminded her she had rented the car and had listed herself as the sole driver, a legality Ali was willing to overlook in exchange for some much needed sleep. Apparently Garrett wasn't.

Though she'd repeatedly asked him their final destination, the most she had been able to get out of him was that he'd arranged for them to stay in a friend's hunting cabin.

"I feel like I'm playing connect the dots," she said wearily, as she made the turn off the highway that carried them beneath an iron arch bearing the brand CCC. "Turn here, turn there. Go straight. At least tell me if we're getting close."

"We're almost there. Keep driving until you see a small wooden arrow on the right that says 'Hunting Cabins.'"

"Are you sure these people are expecting us?" she asked uneasily. "It's four o'clock in the morning. I don't want somebody shooting at me, thinking I'm a trespasser."

"They know we're coming."

"Have you been here before?"

"Once." He pointed ahead. "There's the sign."

Ali made the turn, slowing when her headlights illuminated a road that was little more than a path. "Now I know why you told me to request an SUV from the rental agency."

"Pointless to hide, if you're going to make yourself easily accessible."

"I shouldn't even be hiding," she said petulantly. "I should be at home asleep in my bed."

"If you were home, I guarantee you wouldn't be sleeping. You'd be listening to your doorbell and phone ring off the wall. And if those guys hanging around outside have figured out a way to scale the rock wall that borders the street-side of your property, you might find yourself staring at a stranger's face in your window—or worse, the lens of a camera. And when daylight arrives, you can bet at least one helicopter will be hovering over your house, taking aerial shots." He waved a dismissive hand. "But once those pictures hit the papers, you wouldn't have time to worry about the cameras any longer. You'd be too busy trying to stay alive."

"Okay, okay," she snapped. "I get your point."

"Good. I really don't want to have this conversation again."

She saw a large shadow looming ahead and hit the bright lights. "Is that the cabin?" she asked.

"One of them."

"How many are there?"

"Six, as I recall. They've left the cabin on the far end open for us."

She'd driven past two, when he said, "It's the next one"

"But you said there were six," she said in confusion.

"At least that many. But there are only three on this particular road.".

She pulled to a stop, and glanced in the rearview mirror at the path they'd followed, barely visible in the red glow of her brake lights. "You call that a road?"

He climbed from the vehicle. "Accessibility," he reminded her.

"Yeah, yeah," she grumbled, as she trudged toward the rear of the SUV to help him with the bags. An eerie howl sounded in the distance and sent her scurrying to Garrett's side. "Did you hear that?" she asked in a nervous whisper.

"Hear what?"

The howl sounded again. *"That,"* she said, with a shudder.

He pushed her tote against her chest, forcing her to take it. "Probably a coyote."

"Probably?" With her gaze fixed on the darkness, she eased closer to his side. "You aren't sure?"

He pulled out her suitcase and set it on the ground. "You're the one from Texas. Don't you know a coyote when you hear one?"

"Sorry," she said dryly, "but we don't have many coyotes roaming the streets of downtown Austin."

He closed the rear hatch and the interior light blinked off, leaving them in inky darkness. He tried to turn, but with Ali on one side and her suitcase on the other, he was trapped.

"If you'll give me some room," he said in frustration, "I'll lead the way to the cabin."

She grabbed the handle of her suitcase and dragged it out of his path, but remained where she was. "No way, buster. You're not leaving me to bring up the rear. The last person on the trail is always the one plucked off and never seen again."

He heaved a sigh. "I'm sure there's logic in there somewhere, but I'm too damn tired at the moment to reason it out."

With Ali sticking to him like glue, he made his way to the cabin. Once inside, it didn't take Ali long to figure out the cabin had only one bed, which she was quick to point out to Garrett.

"So we'll share," he replied. "It's a king. It's certainly big enough."

"Both of us in the same bed?"

He shrugged off his jacket and tossed it to a chair. "If you have a problem sharing, you can sleep on the couch."

She glanced through the doorway at the couch in the other room, thinking about the eerie howling she'd heard, as well as the lunatic who supposedly wanted Garrett dead. Deciding that sleeping on the couch held about as much appeal as being the last person on the trail, she snatched up pillows and began erecting a wall down the center of the bed.

"Line of demarcation," she warned him.

Ali didn't expect to sleep a wink. Not with the threat of an assassin on her mind and Garrett on the other side of the bed. To her surprise, within minutes of closing her eyes, she slipped into a deep sleep and didn't stir until hours later, when sunlight flooding through the bedroom window pricked at her eyelids. In an effort to block the sun, she folded an arm over her head and snuggled deeper into the cocoon of bedding.

Her mind slowly registered a difference in the firmness of the wall of pillows at her back, as well as the heat it was producing. Praying the cause wasn't what she feared, she cautiously pushed her buttocks against the wall and froze when she met the unmistakable shape and resistance of an erection.

"Don't panic," a sleepy voice said from behind her. "Men wake up like this all the time."

She twisted around to find Garrett directly behind her. "And that's supposed to make me feel better?"

"Only if you considered it a threat." He lifted a shoulder. "But if you prefer to claim ownership for producing it...."

"Claim ownership?" she repeated, then sputtered a laugh and rolled from the bed, pleased to discover he had a sense of humor. "As if."

"Where are you going?" he called after her.

"To get dressed."

"Don't you want to finish what you started?"

She fluttered a hand, but kept walking. "No, thanks."

After dressing, Ali went to the kitchen in search of food, and found Garrett sitting at the table in the breakfast nook, working at his laptop. "Have you eaten?" she asked, as she passed him on her way to the refrigerator.

"Nibbled."

"Well, nibbling's not going to cut it for me. I'm starving." She opened the refrigerator and was surprised to find it fully stocked. "Wow. Your friends really know how to make a person feel welcome."

"Mandy likes to play mother."

She froze, her hand on a bowl of fruit. *Mandy?* Forcing the tension from her shoulders, she pulled out the bowl of fruit. "I, uh, assumed your friend was a male."

"Mandy is Jase's wife. They're both friends."

A pitifully brief explanation, but at least she now knew this Mandy person wasn't a romantic interest of Garrett's.

Not that she cared, she told herself.

She dropped down on the chair opposite him and plucked a grape from the bowl. "What are you doing?" she asked curiously.

"Checking my e-mail."

"You can get Internet access in the boonies?" she asked doubtfully.

He tapped a finger against the side of his laptop. "Thanks to a wireless card from my cell phone provider. Anywhere I can receive cell phone reception, I can access the Internet."

"Wow!" She popped the grape into her mouth, chewed. "So? Any word on the guy who's threatened you?"

"No."

"Have you checked to see if you've made the news?"

"No mention, yet."

"Well, that's good, isn't it? It means we're safe here, right?"

"For the time being."

Grimacing, she fished a strawberry from the bowl. "You could've lied, you know," she informed him, as she sank her teeth into the strawberry. "I could use some reassurance here."

"I'm not going to lie just to ease your mind." He closed the lid of his laptop and met her gaze. "But if it'll make you feel better, the more time that passes without my whereabouts making the news, the more likely it is the person who's threatening me will fall into the trap my security team has set for him."

"You consider that reassuring?" With a woeful shake of her head, she rose. "If that's the best you can do, I'm pulling a Scarlett O'Hara."

"What's a Scarlett O'Hara?"

"Putting off until tomorrow what I don't want to think about today."

"What does that resolve?"

"Nothing for you, maybe," she told him as she moved to the den, "but it works wonders for me." She stopped before the fireplace to look at the portrait hanging above it. "Who're they?" she asked curiously.

"Jase's parents."

"They look nice," she said.

"I wouldn't know. I never met them."

"Sometimes you can tell a person's personality just by looking," she said, studying the couple's faces. "Look at her smile. It's not just on her lips, it's in her eyes. And him," she said, pointing. "The way he's holding his arm around her, his stance? He obviously adores her and is very protective of her."

"That's quite a lot to assume from a simple photograph."

"Some things can't be faked." She ambled on, smoothing a hand over the supple leather of the sofa's back, as she looked around. "This is a cool place.

Rustic, yet comfy. Much nicer than what I'd expect a hunter's cabin to look like."

"This was Jase's home."

She glanced back to find Garrett had moved to stand in the doorway between the kitchen and den, and was watching her.

"Why'd he move?" she asked.

"It was Mandy's idea. After they married, she wanted to live in the family home."

"Family home?" Her imagination conjured a big rambling house full of kids and laughter. "I guess his brothers and sisters didn't have a problem with that?"

He seemed to hesitate a moment, then shook his head. "Jase was the Calhouns' only child. He inherited their entire estate after their deaths."

"Wow," she said and crossed to peer out the front window. "He inherited all this?"

"Yes."

"How big is it?"

"I have no idea. Huge, I would imagine. I know he raises cattle and has a large pecan orchard business, plus he leases hunting rights and cabins to hunters during hunting season. I'd think all that would require a substantial number of acres."

"Probably." She turned to him. "Do you think he'd mind if I wandered around and took some pictures?"

"Of what?"

"Nature, silly," she said, laughing. "There are

some gorgeous old trees behind the cabin, and woods are usually full of all kinds of interesting vegetation."

"I don't think he'd mind, as long as you didn't stray too far."

"Cool!" She started for the bedroom to get her camera, then stopped, remembering the coyote she'd heard howling the night before. "Want to come along?" she asked hopefully.

He pushed away from the wall. "Why not? There's nothing else to do."

She beamed a smile. "Great. I'll get my camera. Won't take a second."

When she returned, Garrett was standing before the gun case, studying its contents. Her blood chilled, as she watched him take out a handgun.

"Uh, what are you doing?" she asked uneasily.

He spun the cylinder, checking the chambers for bullets. "Never know what you might run into in the woods."

"Do you think the guy who's after you will come here?"

He shrugged. "Best to be prepared."

She gulped, wishing she hadn't asked. "Do you know how to shoot a gun?"

He tucked the pistol into the waist of his jeans. "I rescued Zelda."

"Zelda? The video game?"

At his nod, she choked a laugh. "Just my luck. Of

all the men in the world to get marooned with, I get stuck with a computer nerd who thinks he's embodied with super powers."

Garrett sat on a log, watching Ali stroll alongside the creek, snapping pictures.

In spite of the danger lurking somewhere beyond the boundaries of the ranch, he felt surprisingly relaxed, calm even. He'd been living with the threat of his would-be assassin long enough to know that his current mood wasn't normal. He also knew Ali was responsible for the change. She had a way of dealing with adversity that reduced its importance, made the most dire situation seem almost comical.

Pulling a Scarlett O'Hara.

He shook his head in amusement. Leave it to Ali to come up with something like that. But as ridiculous as her method sounded, he couldn't argue its success. Caught in a similar situation, another woman would be wringing her hands and wailing about her plight. Not Ali. In spite of the danger they might be in, she was seemingly having the time of her life, crawling over rocks and stumps, taking pictures of plants and bugs, and all because she refused to think about their problem.

Some might consider her method of dealing with adversity a form of denial, foolish and nonproductive. A week ago, Garrett would have thought the same damn thing. But after spending time with her and experiencing, if only by association, the benefits of her methodology, he was beginning to believe the whole world would be a better place if more people took Ali's approach to life.

"Careful," he called to her, as her foot slipped on a rock. "That water might not be deep, but I'll bet it's cold."

"And icky," she said, making a face, as she looked through the viewfinder. "Lots of moss and slime. Oh!" she squealed. "There's a turtle."

"In the water?"

"Hiding under a rock." She lowered the camera and motioned for him to join her. "Come look."

"Thanks, but I've seen a turtle before."

"Not one this big. He's huge!"

Heaving a sigh, Garrett pulled the pistol from his waistband and set it on the log, before crossing to her.

She lifted the camera strap over her head and dropped it over his. "You can see him better through the zoom lens," she explained. "Hunker down here," she said, pointing to the spot where she'd been standing. "He's on the far side of the creek."

Garrett squatted down and brought the camera before his face. "I don't see anything."

She stooped behind him to peer over his shoulder. "Move the camera a little bit to the left. A little more. Do you see it now?"

He lowered the camera in disgust. "I don't see anything but rocks and muddy water."

"Oh, for heaven's sake," she fussed, and reached over his shoulders to bring the camera before his face again. Placing her cheek next to his, to align their vision, she nudged the camera a fraction to the left. "There. Do you see him now?"

See what? Garrett wasn't sure he hadn't been struck blind. He'd heard of sensory overload before, but he had never personally experienced its debilitating powers. With Ali's breasts hugging the back of his neck like a cushioned collar, her cheek chafing like silk against his, and her strawberry-scented breath teasing his nostrils, all he could think was, with a slight turn of his head, he could taste her strawberry-flavored lips. A quarter turn more, and he could bury his face in the pillowed softness of her breasts.

"Well, do you?" she asked impatiently. She glanced his way, and drew back with a start, when she found him looking at her and not the turtle. Her eyes rounded. "You're feeling it, aren't you?" she cried. "That sizzle of sensation?"

He considered lying, but it seemed pointless to continue to deny what must be obvious.

"Makes you want to test it, doesn't it? See how far we can push it without getting burned."

"Yeah," she breathed, and wet her lips.

Without allowing himself time to think of consequences, he turned on the balls of his feet, caught her face between his hands and stood, bringing her mouth to his. He tasted the strawberries that had teased him moments before, found the lingering sweetness of grapes, before her lips parted beneath his on a sigh, inviting him to deepen the kiss. He did so gladly, exploring the secret crevices, teasing her tongue until it danced with his.

"Sizzling yet?" he murmured against her lips.

"Oh, yeah," she breathed. "How about you?"

He slipped his hands inside her jacket and smoothed his hands up her ribs. "I'm not sure. Describe the sensation to me."

Her breath caught as his thumbs bumped over the fullness of her breasts. "Can't," she said, releasing the breath on a shuddery sigh against his lips. "Brain's fried."

He was afraid his was, too. The curves his hands traced were soft and utterly feminine, her body's response to his touch sensual and arousing. Desire stirred his loins, a none too subtle reminder of how long it had been since he'd been with a woman.

Refocus on the goal. Keep a respectable distance.

He drew back at his conscience's reminder, telling himself he would do both, but one look at her passion-glazed eyes, the moist, swollen lips still poised for a kiss and he knew keeping a distance was no longer an option.

Given time, he probably could've come up with a better way to express his needs, prettier words with which to seduce her. But at the moment, only the simplest came to mind.

"I want you. Now."

A trail of coats, boots, jeans and sweaters stretched from the front door of the cabin to the foot of the king-size bed. Lust left no time for modesty or tidiness. It carried them straight to the bed, where they fell, their mouths welded, their bodies so closely entwined it was impossible to determine where one started and the other stopped.

For Ali it wasn't close enough. She'd never wanted a man as badly as she did Garrett at that moment. Awakening that morning with him spooned at her back probably had a lot to do with her ravenous hunger. But, if she were honest, it had been building since the morning she'd opened her door, taken his hand, and felt that first ripple of awareness crawl up her arm. His appeal had taken a jump the day she was photographing him in his Western gear and she'd seen what a smile did to his face. And the night he'd kissed her in the middle of Interstate 35…well, his lust factor had shot off the charts.

Desperate to touch him, explore every inch of his body, she swept her hands down his back, over his buttocks, dragged them up his arms, marveling at the strength she sensed within each tightly corded muscle. And his chest…oh, his chest, she thought with a shiver, as she splayed her hands over the expanse and pressed a kiss against its center, inhaling the scent of sandalwood. She'd carried the image of his bared chest to bed with her the night before when he'd commandeered her bedroom and had spent sleepless hours awake and yearning.

But there was no need to yearn any longer.

Knotting her fingers in his hair, she returned her mouth to his and teased his tongue into a dance, all but begging him to take her. As if in response to her silent request, he slipped a hand between her thighs, and she had to clamp her knees together to keep from shattering right then and there.

"Let me touch you," he whispered against her lips.

At his urging, she let her legs part and closed her eyes, focusing on each new sensation he evoked as he stroked the velvety folds of her femininity.

No more words passed between them. There was no need for talk. They communicated with their hands, their eyes, conveyed their impatience with low, guttural groans, their pleasure with long, breathy sighs.

She pressed her lips to his throat, his shoulder, his chest, and savored the salt on his skin, his very maleness. Stroked her hands over his back, his arms, his buttocks, and wondered at his endurance. Everywhere their bodies touched burned as her need for him spiraled higher and higher, until she feared it would consume her. Growing impatient, she cupped his buttocks and urged his hips to hers. His sex brushed her center, and she arched, then melted, her womb softening to accept him.

Braced above her, with his eyes locked with hers, he pushed inside. He held himself there for a heartbeat, two, then began to move, each thrust taking him deeper and deeper inside. She watched the passion build on his face, touched her fingers over the flush of it, then dragged her fingertips down to his lips, his chest. With a groan, he dropped his mouth to hers, mimicking with his tongue the thrust of his sex inside her. It proved to be too much for her.

Desperate for the release that teased her, she arched high and hard. Her body seemed to implode, folding in on itself to envelop him, absorbing the tremors that shook him. She closed her eyes and inhaled deeply, sure that she would die from the sheer pleasure of it all. Seconds, maybe hours passed as she floated, completely sated. A hand cupped her cheek and she opened her eyes again to find him looking down at her.

"Ali."

Her name was hardly more than a whisper that slipped past his lips, but the sound of it, the wonder in it, squeezed at her chest. Emotion rose to fill her throat and released a single word to drift through her mind, wing its way to her heart.

Love.

No, she told herself, and squeezed her eyes shut, telling herself it wasn't possible—she couldn't be falling in love with Garrett. She barely knew him. But when she opened her eyes and met the warmth of his, saw the tenderness, the utter contentment of his expression, she knew there was no way she could deny her feelings.

"You okay?" he asked in concern.

She forced a smile and nodded. "Yeah. Fine."

He lowered himself over her to touch his mouth to hers, then nestled his face in the curve of her neck.

Five

It took a moment for Ali's pulse to slow, her mind to clear enough to absorb the magnitude of what had just transpired.

She, Ali Moran, lowly innkeeper of Vista Bed and Breakfast, had just had sex with *the* Garrett Miller.

Not just sex, she thought with a shiver. Mind-blowing, toe-tingling, life-altering sex.

And it had started with nothing more than a kiss. In a matter of seconds the kiss had escalated to a sexual encounter that had blinded her to the fact that Garrett was essentially a stranger. Under normal circumstances, that fact would have kept her from tumbling into bed with a man.

Which further proved her current circumstances were anything but normal. Hiding from a would-be assassin on a ranch God-knew where with a man with whom she had about as much in common with as she did…well, she didn't have anything in common with him, which was exactly the point, and just one more reason to question why she'd all but raced him to bed.

A hand touched her cheek, and she jumped, startled, and turned her gaze to find Garrett looking at her.

"I—" He stopped, then shook his head. "I don't know what to say."

Assuming by his hesitancy, his expression that what he wanted to tell her was that he regretted making love with her, she tried to sit up. "You don't have to say anything. Really. I understand."

He pressed a hand to her chest, stilling her. "No. I don't think you do." He leaned to touch his lips to hers in a kiss so sensual it sent a shiver chasing down her spine. "That was a…surprise."

His voice was husky, the stroke of his thumb along her cheekbone as mesmerizing as the eyes that held hers.

She melted back against the pillow. "Yeah. It was."

"I probably should apologize for taking advantage of you, but if I did, it would be insincere. I'm not one damn bit sorry."

"It wasn't like you forced me."

His mouth curved in a smile. "Which makes it all the more interesting."

"Garrett," she began, then stopped, her mind going blank as he stroked his hand down her throat, cupped a breast.

He lifted a brow. "You know, I think this is the first time I've ever seen you at a loss for words."

She choked a laugh. "You may be right."

"In that case—" he draped an arm over her waist and drew her hips to his "—I know something we can do that doesn't require words."

Of the same mind, she looped her arms around his neck. "I'm game."

A muffled ring had Ali sleepily lifting her head. Realizing it was her cell, she scrambled from the bed, where she and Garrett had spent the greater part of the last two days, and dug her phone from her tote bag. "Hello?"

"Where *are* you?"

Wincing, she sank down on the foot of the bed. "Hey, Traci."

"Don't 'hey, Traci' me. Where are you?"

"I'm—" She glanced at Garrett, who was awake, too, and listening. "Out of town," she finished vaguely.

"Well, you might have told me you were moving," Traci said, with a sniff. "I am your best friend, after all."

"Moving?" Ali repeated in confusion. "I didn't say anything about moving. I said I'm out of town."

"Then why is there a For Sale sign in front of your house?"

Ali shot up from the bed. "What?" she cried.

"A For Sale sign. I saw it when I went over there this morning. After you didn't show up for yoga class," she added.

Ali dropped her head to her hand. "Oh God, Traci. I'm sorry. I totally forgot about yoga."

"Along with telling me you were moving," Traci said, sounding hurt. "And what is it with all those people hanging around your house? When I went by to check on you, these guys rushed my car. Scared me to death. I took off so fast, it's a wonder I didn't run over somebody."

Ali flattened her lips. "As far as I'm concerned, you could have run them all down. They're tabloid photographers."

"No kidding? Are they there because of your mystery guest?"

"No," she said wryly, "they want pictures of me." She dragged a hand over her hair. "Back to the For Sale sign," she said refocusing the conversation. "Some kid must have put it there as a prank."

"Juvenile delinquents," Traci said testily. "You'd think they'd have something better to do with their time, than terrorizing the neighborhood."

"I probably should call the Realtor and let them know. Do you remember the name of the company on the sign?"

"It was one of those national chains. Century 21, I think."

"Great," Ali muttered. "There's probably a dozen or more Century 21 offices in Austin."

"I'd offer to drive by and get the name for you, but those guys who are hanging around scare me."

"Me, too," Ali agreed, then shook her head. "Don't worry about it. I'll make a few calls and see what I can find out."

"Allbright," Traci blurted out. "I remember now. It was Allbright Century 21."

"Well, that's handy. You just saved me making a dozen calls."

"What about your houseguest?" Traci asked. "Did you just leave him at the house to fend for himself?"

"Uh, no." Ali shot a glance over her shoulder at Garrett. "He's with me."

"What! You mean y'all are *together?*"

Ali rose and walked away from the bed. "Sort of," she said in a voice low enough she hoped Garrett couldn't hear.

"Details, girlfriend. I want details."

"Later. I have to go."

"No!" Traci cried. "Not until you tell me where you are."

"Sorry. No can do."

"Ali Moran, don't you dare—"

Ali disconnected the call, cutting Traci off, then blew a breath up at her bangs.

"Problem?"

She turned to find Garrett sitting up in bed, the covers bunched at his waist. How he could look so mouthwateringly *good* after so many days of nonstop sex was beyond her. Personally she felt—and probably looked—like a rag. She crossed to crawl onto the bed. "Traci's mad at me because I didn't show up for yoga."

"Traci?"

"Girlfriend."

"What was that I heard about moving?"

"When I didn't show up for yoga, she went by the house to check on me and saw a For Sale sign out front." She lifted a shoulder as she settled at his side. "School's out for the holidays, so it was probably some kid pulling a prank."

"You should notify the Realtor."

"I will."

"I take it our friends are still hanging around?"

She hid a smile. "Traci said she was afraid she'd run over one of them."

"Too bad she didn't."

"I'll tell her to work on her aim." Her smile slowly faded, as she wondered what their presence meant. "Since they're still there, does that mean we're safe?"

"It's best to assume we're not." Her expression must have revealed her disappointment, because he gave her leg a reassuring pat. "Tell you what. You call the Realtor about your For Sale sign, and I'll call my security chief and check to see what's happening in Switzerland."

"Deal."

While Garrett went for his phone, Ali called directory assistance for the number of the realty company, then waited for the connection.

"Allbright, Century 21. May I help you?"

"I hope so," she said, heaving a sigh. "One of your For Sale signs is in front of my house. A kids' prank, I'm sure, but I thought your company would want to know so they can return it to the property it was taken from."

"Yes, we certainly do, and I'm so sorry for the inconvenience. The address?"

Ali rattled off the Vista's street address. "Kids," she said, and chuckled. "They do the darnedest things."

"By chance are you Ali Moran?"

"Well, yes," Ali said in surprise. "How did you know?"

"I just checked our database, and we have that property listed for sale. Your name is listed as the contact."

"No. You're mistaken. I'm not selling the Vista."

"You may not be, but the owner is. Mr. Ronald Fleming. In fact, the listing agent has been trying to reach you all morning to make arrangements to show the property. If you'll hold, I'll connect you with Diane. She's the listing agent."

Ali dropped the phone to her lap, breaking the connection. No, she told herself numbly. This had to be a mistake. Ronald Fleming didn't own the house. Ali did. Mimi had given it to Ali, because she knew her son didn't care a flip about the house and would sell it at the first opportunity.

"Ali?"

She looked up to find Garrett looking at her in concern.

"What's wrong?" he asked. "Did you talk to the Realtor?"

She nodded, not trusting her voice. "She said it wasn't a prank. Mimi's son listed the house."

He sank down on the edge of the bed. "But you said Mimi gave you the house."

Tears filled her eyes. "I thought she did."

He stared at her a long moment, then squeezed her knee. "It's probably just a misunderstanding. Why don't you call her attorney. I'm sure he can straighten it out."

She shook her head. "I don't know her attorney's name. The only person I know to ask is Claire." She glanced at the bedside clock and her shoulders drooped. "And I can't call her now. It's the middle of the night in Australia."

She drew in a steadying breath, refusing to believe there was even a chance her house was about to be sold out from under her. "I'm sure you're right," she said, trying to think positively. "It's probably just some crazy misunderstanding." She forced a smile. "So? What did you find out from your security guy?"

"The trap is set. They're just waiting for him to take the bait."

"And when will that happen?"

"Hopefully within the next forty-eight hours."

She gave him a hesitant look. "They're sure he's in Switzerland and not on his way to Texas?"

"He was seen entering a Swiss hotel less than two hours ago."

"And they'll let you know if there's a change, right?"

"Without question." He gave her knee another pat and rose. "I don't know about you, but I'm starving. Let's get something to eat."

She had a feeling his mention of food was just a ruse to get her mind off the danger they were in, as well as her uncertainties concerning the ownership of the Vista, but she was grateful for the distraction.

"It's nice out," she said, and scooted from the bed. "Let's make a picnic lunch."

Garrett didn't know whether to curse himself for not following up with his lawyer concerning ownership of the Vista or breathe a huge sigh of relief, as he and Ali hiked through the woods.

He ended up breathing a sigh of relief.

If he *had* followed up and discovered the property was owned by Ronald, he would have instructed his lawyer to purchase the Vista, which meant that he would be the current owner, not Ronald and he would be the one responsible for Ali's earlier state of despair.

That he would care about Ali's feelings or that he was responsible for them was new and a complication he refused to think about…for the time being, anyway.

Setting the thoughts aside, he spread the blanket over the ground at the picnic spot Ali had chosen. "Hard to believe it's January," he said, as he spread the blanket over the ground. "At home they're shoveling snow."

Ali sank down and began removing items from the basket of food she'd packed for them. "I can't say I miss winters up north."

He shrugged off his jacket, before joining her on the blanket. "It's got to be close to seventy degrees."

"Probably." She popped a strawberry into her mouth and smiled, as she chewed. "And tomorrow could be below freezing. It's best not to question Mother Nature, just enjoy her idiosyncrasies."

Chuckling, he stretched out, propping himself up on an elbow. "Which is my policy with most women."

She held a grape before his mouth. He caught the

fruit between his teeth, nipping at her fingers before drawing it into his mouth. "Wasn't Nero merrily eating grapes while Rome burned?"

"Worse. He was playing the fiddle. Men," she said, with a dramatic roll of her eyes. "They're clueless."

"I resent that remark."

She teased him with a smile. "With the proper persuasion I might be convinced to make you an exception."

He cupped a hand behind her neck and brought her mouth to his.

Humming lustfully, she slowly withdrew. "Okay. You get a pass."

Grinning, she handed him a plastic wrapped sandwich, then selected one for herself. She took a bite, chewed. "Tell me about your family," she said.

"Like what?"

"Like mother, father, siblings." She teased him with a smile. "Or were you hatched?"

"Although I've been accused of being inhuman on more than one occasion, I did have a mother and father. Both of whom are now deceased."

She gave him a sympathetic look. "Sorry. Was it recent?"

"My mother died years ago. I have no memory of her. My dad died about three years ago. Cancer."

"Siblings?"

"An only child."

She lifted a brow. "Really? Me, too." She licked mayonnaise from her finger, before lifting the sandwich for another bite. "So were you and your dad close?"

"No."

His clipped, one-word response had her lowering the sandwich to stare. "Did he beat you or something?"

He snorted. "That would've required him to get near me, and I don't recall him ever being within an arm's reach."

She set her sandwich aside. "Seriously?"

"Seriously."

"But—" She stopped, frowned. "He was your only parent. Who took care of you?"

"The first couple of years after my mother died, baby-sitters. When I was six, he remarried."

"What was your stepmother like?"

"An angel."

She blinked, surprised by the transformation in his face as well as his voice, when he spoke of his stepmother. "Tell me about her."

"Kind. Selfless. Intelligent." He lifted a shoulder. "I'd do anything for her."

She stared, not doubting for a minute that he would and wondering what kind of person instilled that kind of devotion. Shaking her head, she picked up her sandwich again. "You were lucky."

"Lucky?"

She took a bite, chewed. "Yeah. I mean, bummer about your dad, but at least you had a good stepmother."

He dropped his head back and laughed.

She lowered her sandwich. "What?"

"Bummer?" He laughed even harder. "I've received all kinds of reactions to my dad's unfatherlylike behavior, but never 'bummer.'"

She jutted her chin. "If you're expecting pity from me, you won't get it. Your father may have been emotionally handicapped, but your stepmother obviously knew a thing or two about parenting and you were darn lucky to have her."

"No one knows that better than me. It's just that your response was so unexpected, so polar opposite of how most people react to hearing about my childhood…. It just struck me as funny."

Pursing her lips, she picked up her soda. "Well, I'm glad you find me entertaining."

He reached to cover her hand with his. "I'm not laughing at you, Ali," he said quietly. "Quite the opposite in fact. I find you refreshing. Fascinating. Intriguing."

She rolled her eyes. "Oh, please. Much more of your bull and I'll need boots."

"That was no bull. It's the truth. You're all those things and more."

She frowned at him, trying to decide if he was

serious. Finding nothing but sincerity in his eyes, she drew her hand from beneath his. "Don't complicate this any more than it is," she warned.

"What do you mean?"

"I *mean,* this situation is already packed with enough drama to keep a soap opera's scriptwriters in material for a year. Being stalked by the media," she said, ticking off items on her fingers. "Marooned in a secluded cabin in the woods. A would-be assassin on the loose. Living with the possibility of having my house sold out from under me at any moment."

"And me finding you fascinating complicates those things?"

"Well, of course it does!" she cried. "I'm at my most vulnerable right now. Falling for you would be a huge mistake."

"Why?"

"You need to ask?" she asked incredulously.

"Obviously I do."

"Because you're a zillionaire, and I'm an innkeeper who might not even have an inn to keep when and if I make it back home. You live on the East Coast, I live in Central Texas. You're left-brained, I'm right. Making love with you is absolutely incredible. February 1, you're gone."

"Obviously you've given this some thought."

Embarrassed because she had, she dropped her

gaze. "If I don't allow myself to believe something is possible, then I can't be disappointed when I'm proven right."

"Ah, Ali," he said softly. "Only you could come up with a rationale like that."

"There's nothing wrong with my reasoning."

"No," he agreed, "not a thing." He sat up and tugged her over, burying his face in the curve of her neck. "So what's the plan?"

Distracted by his sensual nibbling at her neck, she asked weakly, "What plan?"

"For the remainder of the month. For us."

She turned in his arms. "Enjoy every minute of every day." Smiling, she pressed her mouth to his and forced him back to the blanket. "And *you*."

Garrett couldn't argue with Ali's plan. The company of a beautiful and fascinating woman, and the promise of unlimited and unbelievable sex for a month, with absolutely nothing expected from him in return? Hell, it was every man's fantasy!

He did suffer a moment's concern when he considered the future. Ali was his stepmother's daughter, after all. What would happen when the month was over and she discovered his stepmother was *her* mother?

He pushed the worrisome thought away, telling himself he'd deal with that problem later. It wasn't as if she had any expectations of a future with him, he reminded himself. She, herself, had offered up a laundry list of reasons as to why a relationship with him would never work. She'd even told him she intended to enjoy the time they had together. So why should he feel guilty about taking advantage of what she so freely offered?

He glanced over his shoulder at the cabin where Ali was inside placing a call to her friend Claire in Australia. He didn't even want to think how that conversation would affect Ali. Her love for the big, rambling house was obvious. She'd spent, what, ten years in the house? Caring for it, maintaining it, building a business around it. She was bound to take losing it hard, especially after thinking it was hers. What bothered him was how she would take the news.

So why was he standing outside, avoiding going inside the cabin? he asked himself. The answer was so clear, a blind man could have seen it. He didn't want Ali hurt, didn't want to see the heartbreak in her eyes, on her face. Didn't want to see any more evidence of the victim he'd begun to believe she was.

Heaving a sigh, he forced himself to take that first reluctant step toward the cabin.

Ali tugged up the hem of her shirt to mop her eyes. "It's okay," she assured Claire tearfully. "And please don't think I blame Mimi. It's not like she knew she was going to die. She probably thought she had plenty of time to change her will."

"But you know she didn't want Dad to have the house," Claire argued stubbornly. "She knew he didn't care anything for it, would just sell it. That's why she wanted you to have it."

Ali gulped back tears, nodded. "I know, and I wish it was mine. I hate to see it sold, as much as Mimi would if she were here."

"Oh, Ali," Claire cried softly. "If there was any way I could stop him, you know I would."

"I know, Claire. I know. But what's done is done. There's no use either one of us crying over it now."

"Why don't you buy it?" Claire said impulsively.

"Me?" Ali choked a watery laugh. "Don't I wish. But you know what property values are like in Austin, especially those around downtown. I could never afford to buy the Vista." She drew in a steadying breath, searching for the positive thoughts she needed to get her through this. "I've had ten wonderful years at the Vista, thanks to you and Mimi. For that I'll always be grateful."

"Oh, Ali," Claire wailed. "I could just wring Dad's neck. He's so heartless, so *mean.*"

"Don't blame your dad," Ali scolded gently. "He can't help being the way he is."

"Like hell he can't," Claire muttered bitterly. "You'd think he would've inherited at least *some* of

Mimi's heart. But, no, he's just like Papa Fleming. Selfish and mean to the bone."

"I guess it skipped a generation," Ali said. "You definitely have Mimi's heart." She drew in another breath. "I better go. I've kept you on the phone long enough."

"I'm so sorry, Ali-Cat," Claire said miserably, falling back on the nickname she'd given Ali during their college years. "If there's anything I can do, just let me know, okay?"

"I will. Love you," she said and quickly disconnected. Dropping the phone, she buried her face in her hands and gave in to the tears she'd suppressed.

She'd cry just this once, she promised herself. Grieve for the house she'd grown to love, the home it had become for her, the living it had provided her. Then she'd put it behind her. Not think about it again. Pull herself up by the bootstraps and figure out what to do, where to go. But she needed this moment of self-pity, this opportunity to rail at the fates who seemed to have had it in for her since birth.

What had she done to deserve so much disappointment, so much grief? she asked herself, letting the tears fall. Conceived by parents who didn't want her and given to parents who only wanted someone to carry on their precious family tradition of becoming doctors. And when her adoptive parents had turned their backs on her and all but kicked her out on the streets, had she joined the talk show circuit, crying and whining about her sorry lot in life and the psychological damage inflicted upon her? No, she'd moved to Texas, made a home for herself here, grown to love the state, the city, as well as her home, which she depended on for her support.

And for what? she sobbed, giving in to the resentment, the bitterness. To have it yanked out from under her and be without a home again.

"Ali?"

She snapped up her head to find Garrett standing in the doorway. She leaped to her feet, embarrassed that he'd caught her hosting a pity party for one. "Sorry," she said, scraping her hands across her face. "Got kind of teary-eyed there for a minute."

"Bad news?"

"Yeah. Seems Mimi never got around to changing her will." She gulped, trying to swallow the tears, but they spilled over her lashes.

"Hey," he said softly and crossed to wrap his arms around her.

The offer of comfort was too unexpected, too needed to refuse. She buried her face against his chest. "It's just not fair," she sobbed. "Mimi wanted me to have the house. She really did."

"I'm sure she did."

"And that dumb son of hers couldn't care less. He's been pressuring her for years to get rid of it. He never understood the sentimental value it held for Mimi, how much of her heart was in that house."

"But you did."

She curled her hand into a fist against his chest. "Of course, I did! It was a wedding present from her first husband. He surprised her with it. Planned to live there with her forever. Raise their children there. Then he died. It's full of their love, the memories they made there together. You only have to walk through a room to feel it, to know how much they loved each other, to know how much losing him cost her."

He held her, rubbing a hand up and down her back to soothe, until she'd cried herself out.

She gulped, swallowed, then turned away, afraid if she continued to let the grief hold her she'd never be able to stop crying. "Sorry. I didn't mean to fall apart like that."

"I'd say you're entitled."

She nodded, swallowed again "Yeah. But I'm done now." To prove it, she turned and forced a smile. "So? Want to raid the refrigerator and see what we can find for dinner?"

Six

Garrett didn't know which was worse. Watching Ali cry or watching her pretend her world wasn't falling apart. Both were heartbreaking to witness.

He sat in the leather overstuffed chair opposite the sofa, his laptop open before him, watching her leaf through a magazine. She wasn't seeing whatever was on the pages. She might be *looking* at them, but her mind was on something else entirely. The tiny furrow of worry between her brows was a dead giveaway that her thoughts weren't focused on the magazine's glossy pages, but on what troubles awaited her in Austin.

"Have you considered buying the property yourself?" he asked.

She glanced up, as if startled by the sound of his voice, then dropped her gaze to the magazine again and flipped a page. "Can't afford it."

"How do you know, when you haven't applied for a loan?"

"Trust me. I know. You've looked for land in the Austin area. You know that property within the city limits of Austin is at premium. What's around Town Lake is like gold."

Frustrated, he set his laptop aside and stood. "Ask for a business loan. Base your ability to make the payments on the bed-and-breakfast's potential income."

She stared up at him a long moment, as if considering, then dropped her gaze again, shaking her head. "Good idea, but it would never fly. They'd want a down payment of some kind, and I have nothing to offer, other than a paltry savings account."

"But you can't know what they'd want until you try," he argued.

She looked up at him and gave him a halfhearted smile. "I appreciate the suggestion, Garrett, as well as your concern, but I have to be realistic. Building false hope would only make the disappointment that much greater when I was turned down for the loan. And they would turn me down," she said firmly. "I may not have your business experience, but I know enough to know I would never qualify for a loan the size needed to buy the Vista."

"But—"

A knock at the door had him spinning around. He swallowed a groan, when he saw Mandy peering at him through the window.

"Is that your friend?" Ali asked from behind him.

"Yeah," he said, and headed for the door, dread knotting his stomach. "That's her."

Before he had a chance to open the door completely, Mandy was breezing inside, wearing a mile-wide smile and carrying a plastic cake carrier.

"Hi, Garrett!" She blew a kiss in his direction, but kept going and didn't stop until she was standing opposite the sofa and Ali.

She set the cake carrier on the coffee table, then stood and extended her hand in greeting. "Hi, I'm Mandy."

Ali unfolded her legs from beneath her and rose, a smile spreading on her face. "Hi, Mandy. I'm Ali."

"I thought y'all might be craving something sweet," Mandy said, then laughed and gave her rounded belly a pat. "Junior always is." She flapped a hand. "Anyway, I was baking a cake, and thought I might as well bake two and bring y'all one. Do you like chocolate?"

"Are you kidding?" Ali said, laughing. "I'm a woman, aren't I?" She scooped up the cake carrier and headed for the kitchen. "I'll cut us all a piece. Would you like a glass of milk with yours, Mandy?" she called over her shoulder.

"Yes, please," Mandy replied, then turned to Garrett and dropped her jaw, mouthing, "She's darling!"

He narrowed his eyes in a look that promised death if she dared spill the beans about who he was or how he and Mandy were related. "Is there any coffee?" he called to Ali.

"Probably enough for a cup."

He gave Mandy a last warning look, then ducked around her and headed for the kitchen. "I'll make a fresh pot."

"I'll make it," Ali offered.

He cut a glance her way, as he pulled the container of coffee grounds from the cupboard. "I better. Looks like you've got your hands full."

Grinning, she licked chocolate from the tips of her fingers. "One of the perks of cutting the cake. I get whatever icing sticks to me." She levered a slice onto a plate, added a fork. "Would you mind getting the milk?" she asked Garrett, as she cut another wedge.

"I will," Mandy said, as she joined them in the kitchen.

"By the way," Ali told her, "thanks for stocking the refrigerator. I was starving when we woke up that first day and was relieved when I discovered a trip to town wasn't going to be required before I could eat."

Mandy set the carton of milk on the counter and flapped a hand. "Glad to do it. It's not often we have the opportunity to entertain f—"

Garrett bumped her arm and gave her a warning look.

"—friends," Mandy finished, then stuck her tongue out at him behind Ali's back. "Do you want milk, Ali?" she asked, as she poured a glass.

"Yes, please."

Mandy poured a second glass and carried them to the table. "This is so cool," she said as she settled in a chair. "It's not often I get to spend the afternoon eating chocolate cake and talking girl talk."

Garrett pulled out a chair, purposely placing himself between Mandy and Ali. "Me, either," he said dryly.

"I would have dropped by for a visit sooner," Mandy said, "but I've had carpenters at the house all week. We're converting the bedroom next to ours into a nursery and I promised Jase I'd keep an eye on them. They're excellent craftsmen," she was quick to add, then chuckled. "It's just that they have a tendency to drag a job out forever, if you don't prod them along."

"Your husband's out of town?" Ali asked curiously.

"He's in Washington, D.C., visiting his mother. But he'll be home tonight," she added. She lifted her fork to her mouth and gave Garrett a mischievous smile over it. "When he heard Garrett was here and had brought a friend to visit, he decided to cut his trip short."

"How nice," Ali said and smiled at Garrett. "You'll get to spend some time with your friend."

"Yeah," Garrett said, that knot of dread twisting tighter in his stomach at the thought of Jase coming home. "Nice."

Ali shifted her gaze from Garrett to Mandy. "How did y'all meet? You and Garrett, I mean."

"College—"

"Mutual friend—"

Garrett and Mandy exchanged a glance as their voices tangled and their explanations clashed. Mandy popped a piece of cake into her mouth and waved her fork at Garrett, indicating for him to explain.

"A mutual friend from college introduced us," he said, praying Ali would leave it at that. He figured the fewer lies he had to tell, the less chance he and Mandy—and later, Jase—would have of getting their stories mixed up.

"Oh," Ali said, seeming satisfied with his explanation, then shifted her attention to Mandy and smiled. "So, when is your baby due?"

That sent the conversation in a whole new direction and left Garrett breathing a sigh of relief.

For the moment.

"Mandy's nice."

Garrett climbed into bed and stretched out beside Ali. "Yeah. She is."

"I can't believe she's so big, and she's only four months along."

"She's big all right."

"I wonder if she's carrying twins," she said thoughtfully.

"The two of you talked about everything else," he said dryly. "I'm surprised you didn't ask."

She laughed softly. "I wanted to, but I was afraid I might hurt her feelings. You know. Like I was saying she was fat or something."

"She is fat."

"She is not," she scolded. "She's pregnant. There's a difference."

He rolled to his side to face her, and plumped his pillow beneath his head. "If you say so."

Smiling, she snuggled close. "What's her husband like?"

"Jase?"

She lifted a brow. "She has more than one?"

He rolled his eyes. "He's a nice guy, I guess."

"Well, that's certainly descriptive."

"He's a cowboy. You know the type. Tall. Lanky. Wears a hat and boots all the time. Walks slow, talks slow."

Growing thoughtful, she brushed a lock of hair from his forehead. "It's hard to imagine you having a friend like that. I mean. Well, you know. You being a zillionaire computer geek and all."

He drew back to look at her. "What is it with this zillionaire tag you keep sticking me with?"

"Millionaire, zillionaire. When you have a bank balance like mine, all those 'aires' are the same."

He snorted. "Believe me, being wealthy isn't what it's cracked up to be."

"Really?" She snuggled closer. "Tell me what it is like."

"A pain, if you want the truth. Overnight, you become everybody's best friend. People you've never even heard of start coming out of the woodwork wanting something from you. A loan. A partner in a new venture. A job." He shook his head. "You learn real quick that it isn't *you* they're interested in. It's your money."

She trailed a finger down his jaw, her lips puckered in sympathy. "Bummer."

"Yeah. Bummer. And everything about your life changes. You live in a fishbowl, your every move watched and speculated on. Your past becomes an open book, with people digging around to find out all your dirty secrets."

She teased him with a smile. "And what skeletons do you have rattling around in your closet, Mr. Miller? How many secrets are you hiding?"

The stab of guilt hit him square between the eyes and without warning. Only one, he thought, and the person who stood to suffer the most from it lay opposite him.

Stretching over her, he switched out the bedside lamp, wanting the shroud of darkness in which to hide his lie. "I don't have any secrets," he said.

"Ah, come on. Everybody has a secret or two they keep hidden from the world."

"You already know mine."

"What? About your dad?"

"Only a select few know what my childhood was like, and I intend to keep it that way."

"I'm not planning on telling anyone, if that has you worried."

Hearing the hurt in her voice, he draped an arm over her and drew her close. "I never thought you would. I imagine, with parents like yours, you'd understand why I'd prefer no one know what it was like."

"Lonely?"

He thought about that for a minute. "Yeah, although it was years before I realized I was lonely."

"When your stepmother came into the picture."

"Before she came along, I didn't realize I was missing anything. Thought everyone's dad was like mine. Went to work every day, stayed in his office at home until all hours of the night. No hugs good-night. No tossing a ball around in the backyard. No contact. No conversation. No nothing."

She laid her fingers against his cheek and something in his chest shifted at the tenderness in the gesture.

"You wanted his love," she said softly, "were starving for it."

He swallowed hard, never having heard anyone express his need so succinctly or accurately.

"Yeah," he said, and shoved back the image of the little boy who'd gone to sleep every night with a teddy bear hugged to his chest, a lousy substitute for the physical contact, the affection he'd wanted, needed from his dad.

The how-come-I-can't-go pitiful look Ali gave Garrett when he drove away from the cabin made Garrett feel about as low as a snake. But he couldn't very well take her with him to visit Mandy and Jase when she was the purpose of the visit. With Jase home now, he didn't want to take a chance on Jase storming the cabin and demanding that Ali meet their mother, which is exactly what Garrett feared Jase would do. The two men might not be related, and Jase might have come into Barbara's life later than Garrett, but they shared a strong protective instinct when it came to Barbara Jordan Miller.

He figured, too, that he had some explaining to do, since Jase would think, as Mandy had, that Garrett had broken his promise to Barbara about contacting Ali.

As it turned out, his fears were well founded.

He'd barely climbed from the rental, when Jase

came barreling out of the house with murder in his eyes.

Garrett held up a hand to stave off a fight. "I can explain," he said.

Jase halted an arm's length away and dropped his hands to his hips, smoke all but coming out his ears. "You damn well better," he said angrily. "We promised Barb we'd leave Ali alone."

"*You* promised," Garrett corrected. "I promised nothing."

Jase opened his mouth, probably intending to call him a liar, then clamped it shut, obviously realizing that Garrett hadn't made the same promise he and his father, Eddie, had. "You were there when we got back from visiting Ali's parents and knew we were told that Ali wanted nothing to do with her birth family. You heard what Barb said, what she asked of us. She said for us to leave Ali alone."

Garrett nodded. "Yes, and I would've honored her wishes, but I saw how much Barbara wanted to meet Ali, how much it hurt her to know that Ali wanted nothing to do with her. Since I'm not related to Ali, I figured she wouldn't feel the same animosity toward me she might feel toward you or Eddie, if you were to go and see her. I thought I could talk to her, reason with her, convince her to meet Barbara. And, if that failed, I thought I could at least convince her to give Barbara the missing piece of the deed."

"And did you?" Jase demanded.

Garrett grimaced, aware that somewhere along the way, he'd allowed his growing attraction for Ali to distract him from his purpose in being in her home.

"Not yet," he added reluctantly. "My intent was to get to know her first so I'd know how best to gain her cooperation."

"And did you?" Jase asked again.

"No, but I have discovered some things about her that make me believe she'd be willing to meet with Barbara. With all of you."

"By God, she'll meet me," Jase said angrily. "She's on my land, in my cabin. I'd like to see her try leaving this ranch *without* meeting me."

"And that's exactly the kind of attitude that will ruin any chance of reuniting Barbara with Ali." Realizing that his anger had spiked to match Jase's, he drew in a breath through his nose and slowly blew it out. "Which is why I'm here," he said more calmly. "We need to talk."

Jase glared at him a full minute, then spun for the house. "Inside. Mandy'll want to be in on this."

"You're saying the Morans lied?" Jase asked doubtfully.

"I can't say for sure," Garrett replied, "since I haven't confronted Ali directly with anything yet, but, yes, I believe they did." Frowning, he turned his coffee cup slowly between his hands. "I wasn't there when you, Eddie and Barbara visited with the Morans, but I don't remember any of you mentioning Ali being estranged from her adoptive parents."

Jase shook his head. "No. They didn't indicate there were any problems at all."

Garrett scowled. "Well, there are. Big ones. And they go back for years. Ali hasn't seen or spoken to her parents since she moved to Texas ten years ago."

"What!" Jase exchanged a look with Mandy, then turned his attention to Garrett again. "The Morans never let on they weren't in contact with Ali."

"I doubt they would, since they all but kicked her out on the street."

Jase sank back in his chair, clearly unaware of that portion of Ali's past. "Maybe you better explain."

Garrett did, sharing the story of Ali's break with her parents, her move to Texas, just as she'd shared it with him, and finished by telling them about Ronald Fleming inheriting the Vista, instead of Ali.

"Damn," Jase murmured, obviously moved by Ali's plight.

"Yeah," Garrett agreed grimly. "Damn. From what she's told me her life with her adoptive parents was anything but pleasant."

"After meeting the Morans," Jase said grimly, "I'd say the fault lies with them, not Ali."

Garrett nodded. "That's my take on it, too."

"So what do we do now?" Mandy asked. "Just tell her the truth about her past? About Jase being her twin and Barbara wanting to meet her?"

Garrett blew out a breath, shook his head. "I don't know what to do. I want to tell her and plan to. It's the when and how I haven't figured out. It's going to be a shock, no matter how it's handled." He looked at Jase. "Think how you reacted when you were told."

Jase snorted a breath. "I was royally pissed, I can tell you that." He glanced at Mandy. Smiling softly, he reached to take her hand. "If not for Mandy, I probably would've never agreed to meet my father. And without Eddie's input, I doubt I would've ever searched for my mother."

He gave Mandy's hand a squeeze, and turned his attention back to Garrett. "You've spent time with Ali, you know her best. How do you think we should handle telling her?"

"I don't know that there is a good way," Garrett said with regret. "In retrospect, I can see that my going to Austin and using my need for property as an excuse to stay at her bed-and-breakfast, rather than being up-front with her and telling her who I was was a mistake. I'm afraid I've complicated things even more by becoming involved with her."

Jase's eyes sharpened. "Involved?"

Realizing his slip, he dropped his gaze. "We've become…friends. Once she realizes I've deceived her..." He dragged a shaky hand down his face, easily able to imagine her reaction. "Well, I doubt she's going to like me very much, which could make things awkward since we have Barbara in common."

Mandy nodded gravely. "Trust factor. It's important to a woman."

"How about this," Jase suggested. "Bring her over here for dinner. Let me get a feel for the situation, get to know her and her me. Maybe this will be easier than we think."

Garrett considered a moment, then nodded reluctantly, unable to come up with a better plan. "Okay, but give me a few more days with her. Maybe I can find a way to tell her my part in this, before we have to tell her about you being her brother. Feed it to her in small bites. Less of a shock that way."

Ali tried not to pout as she made the bed, but it was hard. She didn't see how her going with Garrett to see his friend Jase would have made any difference. It's not like she would have bellied up to the bar with the men, so to speak, and interfered with their "man talk." She had more sense than that. She could've—and would've, given the chance—spent the time chatting with Mandy.

She smiled at the thought of Mandy, thinking how cute the woman looked with her rounded belly. She doubted Mandy was even aware of the loving way she rubbed her stomach when she talked about the baby. But Ali had noticed and had thought it was about the sweetest thing she'd ever seen. Babies were something out of Ali's realm. Not that she didn't want one some day. She did. She just didn't have any friends who had children and didn't have any experience with infants, or pregnant women for that matter.

Taking a pillow from the bed, she stuffed it under her shirt and turned to the mirror to see what she would look like pregnant. She snorted a laugh at the grotesque shape the pillow formed beneath her shirt as she turned to view her profile.

"What man would love that?" she asked herself, chuckling. She propped her arms over the bump as she'd seen Mandy do, and tried to imagine what it would be like to know a baby was growing inside her, what it would feel like when the baby moved. Would it hurt? Tickle?

She turned to face the front again, wondering how a person could carry a baby for nine months, watch it grow, feel its movements, suffer through its birth, then hand it over to strangers as her mother had done. Had her birth mother cried? she wondered. Had she ever regretted giving Ali away?

Sobered by the thought, she dragged the pillow from beneath her shirt and dropped down on the side of the bed, holding the pillow on her lap. What did her mother look like? she wondered as she smoothed a crease from the fabric. Was her hair blond like Ali's, or had Ali inherited her coloring from her father? Was she tall? Short? Funny? Serious? Were she and Ali's father married? What was she doing now? Where did she live? Did she have other children? Was she rich? Poor? Happy? Sad? Smart? Dumb? A housewife? A career-woman?

Ali dropped her head back, with a groan. How many times had she played this game through the years, asked herself these same questions? And with the same results. There was no way she could know the answers to any of the questions that had haunted her for as long as she could remember, nor would there ever be. Whatever tie she had shared with her mother was severed the day her mother had given her up for adoption.

Blowing out a breath, she dropped her chin to stare at the pillow again. Funny, she thought as she traced a finger over the neat stitches along the seam. She and Garrett had different childhoods, yet they had been similar in many ways. Neither of them had been raised by the woman who had given birth to them. And both of them had parents—or a parent in Garrett's case—who were incapable of loving them and giving them affection.

A wistful smile curved her lips as she imagined Garrett as a young boy when confronted with a step-mother who actually paid attention to him, cared about him. She had never had that. She'd seen loving relationships between her friends and their parents, which is how she knew such a thing existed. It was also how she had come to realize the ache in her chest was due to her not receiving the love and care her friends received.

"And isn't that something?" she murmured. It seemed she and Garrett had something in common after all. They'd both, at one point or another in their lives, been denied love.

Intrigued by the realization, she thought back over the time she'd spent with him and the impressions she'd drawn from each. When he'd first arrived at the Vista, she had thought him an arrogant snob, with an overinflated opinion of himself. She'd also thought him sexy as sin. She sputtered a laugh at the contradiction.

Her smile slowly faded as she realized she no longer thought of him as any of those things—except for the sexy as sin part. All it took was a look or a touch from him and her knees turned to rubber.

With a shiver, she hugged the pillow to her chest, remembering the hours they'd made love. The feel of his hands stroking her body. The way his eyes turned dark with passion, sparkled when he laughed. The pressure of his mouth on hers. His taste. The sense of oneness, completeness, she experienced when they were joined.

She broke off the thought, acutely aware of where her mind was carrying her. She was thinking of their relationship becoming permanent and it was impossible that would ever happen. She might have truly come to care for Garrett. And he may have started to care for her. But men like Garrett fell in love with debutantes and heiresses. Women who shared the same social circle, the same lifestyle. Women who moved gracefully and with style in the world of the wealthy. Men like him didn't fall in love with innkeepers. And they sure as heck didn't marry them.

She pressed a hand over her stomach, already dreading him leaving.

"Are you sick?"

She snapped up her head to find Garrett standing in the bedroom doorway, his forehead furrowed in concern. She released a shuddery breath and stood, laying the pillow aside. "I think I ate too much chocolate cake," she lied.

"Do you need to take something for it? There may be bicarbonate in the medicine cabinet."

She shook her head. "I don't need anything. I'll be okay."

He took her by the elbow and ushered her toward the bed. "Lie down for a while," he said as he pulled back the covers she'd straightened only moments ago. "Maybe you'll feel better after you take a nap."

Helpless to do anything else, she let him guide her into bed.

"Garrett?" she asked hesitantly as he pulled the covers over her.

He shifted his gaze to hers. "What?"

"What kind of women do you normally date?"

He frowned in confusion. "I don't know. Why?"

"No reason. I was just curious."

He considered a moment, then shook his head. "I don't know that I date a certain type. Female. I suppose that's my only requirement. And unattached," he added. "But if you want to know the truth, I seldom have time for dates." He dropped a kiss on her forehead. "Rest a while. I'll be in the den if you need anything."

When he turned to leave, she said, "Garrett?"

He stopped, turned. "What?"

"Will you take a nap with me?"

He hesitated a moment, then crossed back to the bed and toed off his shoes. "You know as well as I do, that if I get in this bed with you, neither one of us are going to sleep."

She flipped back the covers and smiled. "Yeah, I know."

Garrett felt Ali's gaze and glanced over to find her looking at him curiously.

"What?" he asked.

Shaking her head, she turned her gaze back to the path they walked. "Nothing really. I was just wondering why you and Jase haven't spent any time together. Did y'all have a fight or something?"

He released a slow, uneasy breath. He'd worried over a lot of things over the last forty-eight hours, but him and Jase not spending time together sure as hell wasn't one of them. He had racked his brain, trying to think of a way to come clean with Ali, tell her who he was and about her birth family without her hating him. But he still hadn't found any.

Hoping to distract her from what was a reasonable question, he teased her with a smile. "What? Are you trying to get rid of me?"

Laughing, she hugged his arm to her side. "Hardly. I just don't want you sticking close to the cabin because of me. He's your friend and I doubt you get to see each other all that much. You should take advantage of the opportunity while you're here."

That she would consider his needs over her own didn't surprise him and was just another trait she shared with his stepmother.

"I'm sure being out of town put him behind in his work," he said vaguely. "He'll drop by or call when he has a chance."

"If you say so," she said doubtfully. "I just didn't want you thinking you had to baby-sit me."

Knowing he couldn't put off taking her to Jase's house much longer, he stopped on the path and turned her to face him. "If you knew something about someone that they didn't know, would you tell them?"

She sputtered a laugh. "I don't know. I suppose. Why? Do you know something about Jase he doesn't know?"

Dropping his gaze, he smoothed a thumb over her knuckles. "No, though Jase plays a part in it." He looked up at her and opened his mouth, intending to tell her about her birth family as he'd promised Jase he'd do. But then he closed his mouth, knowing if he had a hundred years in which to accomplish the task, he'd never be able to find the words to tell her. Not without her hating him.

And he didn't want Ali to hate him.

Shaking his head, he pulled her into his arms and hugged her tight. "Never mind."

She pushed back to look at him. "But if it's bothering you, I'd like to help."

His smile wistful, he shook his head again. "Thanks, but you can't." He slung an arm around her shoulders and began to walk again. "Tell you what. When we get back to the cabin, I'll call Jase, see if he's caught up yet. I think it's time the two of you met."

Garrett didn't see any way the evening could go well. If he could roll back the clock, he would never have deceived Ali. He'd have told her from the first who he was and why he was at her bed-and-breakfast.

Of course, she may have slammed the door in his face, which would have put them all back at square one, with the family only partially reunited and the missing portion of the deed still missing.

But there was no sense wasting time with regrets, he told himself. What was done was done and he was just going to have to accept how Ali felt about him when this was all over.

"You're awfully quiet. Is something wrong?"

He glanced over at Ali, who was looking at him in concern from the passenger seat.

He turned his gaze back to the road, with a shrug. "No. Nothing to say, I guess."

"It's really nice of Mandy and Jase to have us over for dinner."

"Yeah, it is."

"I wish I'd had something to bring. Flowers. Something. I hate to arrive empty-handed."

"They invited us for dinner. We're not expected to contribute to the meal."

"I know. Still. Mandy stocked the refrigerator for us, brought us that yummy chocolate cake. And she's pregnant. I'd like to do something nice for her."

He slanted her a look. "We don't have to go. We can go back to the cabin if you want."

Her eyes rounded in dismay. "Are you crazy? I want to have dinner with your friends."

"Then why all the fretting?"

She flattened her lips and turned to face the windshield. "Men. Not a social grace in your bodies."

He laughed, in spite of his nervousness about the evening. "We may not have any social graces, but I bet we have fewer ulcers."

She sent him a withering look, then faced the front again. "We'll offer to do the dishes," she decided. "That'll be our contribution to the meal."

"Speak for yourself. I don't do dishes."

"Ingrate," she muttered under her breath, making him laugh.

As he drove up to the house, his smile faded.

"Oh, look," she said in excitement. "They're on the porch waiting for us."

Garrett shifted his gaze to the wide veranda-style porch, where Mandy and Jase sat side by side on a wooden swing. Praying the evening passed without a glitch, he parked and switched off the ignition.

As he climbed from the car, Ali hopped out from the opposite side, waving a hand over her head in greeting.

Mandy and Jase rose and met them at the steps.

Before Garrett had a chance to introduce Ali to Jase, Ali climbed the steps, extending a hand in greeting. "Hi, Jase. I'm Ali."

Garrett watched Jase's face as he shook Ali's hand and was surprised by the amount of emotion he detected in the other man's expression.

"Pleased to meet you, Ali." He released her hand

and stepped aside in an invitation for her to join them. "Mandy and I were just about to have a cup of hot spiced cider. Would you like some?"

"I would. Thanks."

Ali slipped her arm through Mandy's. "I want you to know I hate you. I've polished off at least half that cake."

Laughing, Mandy walked with her to a grouping of wicker chairs. "Better thee than me. I've gained so much weight my OB is threatening to wire my mouth shut."

"Come on, Garrett," Jase said, cutting Garrett off before he could join the women. "You can help me with the cider and leave the women to talk calories and babies."

Once inside, Jase stopped and held a hand against the door.

"You okay?" Garrett asked.

Jase nodded, then drew in a bracing breath and straightened. "It's just weird. Knowing that she and I are twins, yet she's a stranger. A complete stranger."

"Yeah, I'd imagine that's hard to grasp."

"It is," Jase agreed as he led the way to the kitchen. "She seems nice, though. Friendly as a young pup. And she looks so much like Mom, it's spooky."

"Yeah. Took me by surprise, too."

Jase stopped in the doorway and met Garrett's gaze. "We're telling her," he said, his tone brooking no argument. "You can pick the time, but she's not leaving this ranch until she knows she has family who wants to meet her."

Garrett nodded gravely, knowing that in giving Ali her family, there was a strong chance he'd lose her. "Yeah. It's only fair."

Ali walked at Mandy's side, while Mandy toured her through Jase's childhood home.

"It's beautiful," Ali said, awed by the tall ceilings and spacious rooms.

"I've always loved this house," Mandy confessed. "When I was in high school, I worked for Jase's mother here in the home office and I'd dream of living here someday with Jase."

"Really?" Ali said in surprise. "Were you and Jase high school sweethearts?"

"Heavens, no!" Mandy said, laughing. "I was more like his pesky kid sister. Jase was my brother's best friend," she went on to explain. "I had this *huge* crush on him, but he never saw me as anything but Bubba's little sister."

"Obviously he doesn't see you that way anymore. How did the two of you get together?"

"It's a long story," Mandy said as she led the way into the den. She gestured toward the overstuffed sofa. "Let's sit down, and I'll give you the *Reader's Digest* version of our romance."

Mandy tucked a foot beneath her and angled herself on the sofa to face Ali. "I moved back to San Saba after my divorce, wanting to be near family and friends while I adjusted to single life. Jase's mother had passed away a couple of months earlier, and he was in desperate need of someone to take over the office end of his family's businesses. Since I'd had experience working with his mother, he thought I'd be perfect for the job."

"Obviously you were perfect for more than just the job," Ali teased.

"I thought so, too, but it took Jase a while to realize I wasn't a kid any longer, I'd grown up. Even then, he wouldn't commit to a relationship with me." She smiled wistfully, remembering. "I knew he loved me, and I thought I'd made it clear that I loved him, but he'd enjoyed the bachelor life and wasn't ready to give it up. He also had this hang-up about marriage.

"He's adopted, you see," Mandy explained. "And it bothered him that he didn't know who his parents were, what kind of people they were. Of course, I never knew that about him. No one did. He kept it all inside. A doctor would ask him about his parents' health history and it would freak him out because he didn't know.

"He adored Mr. and Mrs. Calhoun," she was quick to add. "He never considered them as anything other than his real parents. It was just when he had to address the fact that he was adopted that caused him problems. He felt like he couldn't get married and have children, when he didn't know anything about himself or what kind of genes he might be passing on."

Ali gave Mandy's stomach a pointed look. "Obviously he got over that."

Smiling, Mandy laid a hand over her belly. "Yes and no. Yes, he decided to get married and have babies, and no he didn't get over his concerns." She seemed to hesitate a moment, then said cautiously, "He met his dad. I think once he saw that his father was normal and not some degenerate, it freed him of whatever concerns he had, and he asked me to marry him."

"Are you telling her about that sorry excuse I have for a dad?" Jase teased as he and Garrett entered the den.

Mandy glanced up and, laughing, held out a hand to Jase. "No, I'm telling her what a sweet and adorable father you have."

Jase dropped down at Mandy's feet and brought her fingers to his lips. "Wouldn't have met him, if not for Mandy. She actually met him first. In fact, she's the one who tracked him down. If left up to me, we'd have never gotten together."

"Really?" Ali said in surprise. "I'd think you would've jumped at the chance to meet your birth father. I know I would."

A silence fell over the room and Ali frowned as

she glanced around and found three sets of eyes focused on her. "What?" she said uneasily. "Did I say something wrong?"

Garrett gave her a nudge and she scooted over, making room for him on the sofa beside her.

"What?" she said again, his somber expression concerning her even more.

"How much do you know about the parents who gave you up?" Jase asked.

She turned to peer at him. "I…well, nothing, really. I know I was born in a hospital in North Carolina, but—" She stopped and looked at him in puzzlement. "How did you know I was adopted?" She glanced at Garrett. "I never even told you."

"No," he said quietly. "You didn't."

"Did your adopted parents ever tell you anything about your birth parents?" Jase asked.

She turned to look at the other man. "Not that I remember. Why?"

"My birth mother wrote me a letter. I thought maybe you were given one, too."

She shook her head, her frown deepening at the oddity of the conversation. "No. All I have is a birth certificate, but my parents' names are listed on it as my mother and father. My adoptive parents," she clarified. "The Morans."

"Does your birth certificate state whether yours was a single birth or multiple?"

She laughed uneasily, shifting her gaze from Jase to Mandy to Garrett. "What is this? An inquisition?"

"No," Jase assured her. "I'm just curious."

"Single," she said, although she couldn't imagine why the circumstances of her birth would be important to him.

Jase exchanged a glance with Garrett that Ali couldn't read.

"What's going on?" she asked in confusion. "I feel like all of you know something I don't."

She felt the weight of a hand cover hers and glanced over at Garrett. Her gut clenched at the grimness of his expression. "Garrett," she said uneasily. "Please tell me what is going on."

"Maybe I should be the one to tell her."

She whipped her gaze to Jase who had made the offer. "Tell me *what?*"

"I've met your adoptive parents, Ali."

She looked at him in confusion. "You've met my parents?"

He nodded. "I went to see them."

She couldn't think, couldn't breathe. None of this made sense. Jase had gone to see her parents? "But…why?"

"I'm a twin."

"So? What does that have to do with me and my parents?"

"I'm *your* twin."

She was on her feet, before she even realized she intended to stand. "What?" she cried, then shook her head. "No. This is crazy." She looked at Garrett for help. "Why is he saying these things? I'm not related to him. I was a single birth." She whipped her head around to glare at Jase. *"Single,"* she repeated, her voice rising. "Not a twin."

He pushed himself to his feet to stand before her. "I don't know why your birth certificate says single birth, but you *are* my twin." He pulled a folded piece of paper from his shirt pocket. "My birth certificate," he said and offered it to her.

She snatched it from his hand and opened it.

The date. The state of issue, North Carolina. The name of the hospital. They were all the same as on her birth certificate. The only differences were the names listed as mother and father.

Even with the proof in front of her, she couldn't believe it was true. "No," she whispered, shaking her head. "You're not my brother. You can't be."

He took the certificate from her trembling hands and tucked it back into his shirt pocket. "I know it's hard to believe. But I am."

"I don't understand." She looked at Garrett. "You knew?"

The guilty look on his face was answer enough.

"But how?" she asked him. "Why?"

"My stepmother is your birth mother," Garrett replied.

The blood drained from her face. "No," she said, and backed away, shaking her head in denial. "No." Hiccupping a sob, she spun and ran from the room.

Jase started after her, but Garrett caught his arm, stopping him. "No. Let me talk to her. I'm the one responsible for this."

Though he could see that Jase wanted to refuse, he finally backed down.

"All right," he said, then leveled a finger at Garrett's nose. "But she's not leaving the ranch. Not until she hears it all."

Seven

The drive back to the cabin was pure torture, with Ali sitting with her shoulder hugged against the passenger door, her face turned to the passenger window. Once inside the cabin, she went straight to the bedroom and began packing.

He laid a hand on her arm. "Ali, let me explain."

She whirled to face him. "Yes, please do. I think I deserve an explanation."

He caught her hand. "Let's sit down."

She yanked free. "I don't want to sit down."

He held up his hands. "All right. Fine. We'll stand." He dropped his arms to his sides. "First, let me say I'm sorry. I never intended for this to turn out this way. I never intended to hurt you. No," he said, shaking his head. "That's not true. I *did* want to hurt you."

She flinched as if he'd struck her, and he reached for her.

"Ali, please."

She took a step back. "No. Don't touch me." She gulped back tears. "You knew. All along, you knew about me, my parents, my adoption. You *knew* your stepmother was my mother, that Jase was my brother, and you never said a word. You told me you were in Austin to look for land. Why, Garrett? Why would you lie to me?"

"It wasn't a lie. I *was* looking for land."

"How convenient," she said, her voice sharp with resentment. "You had to be in Austin anyway, so why not drop by and seduce your stepmother's daughter."

"It wasn't like that, and you know it," he said angrily.

Realizing he was shouting, he stopped and drew in a deep breath, searching for calm. Finding it, he continued. "I didn't tell you who I was because I was afraid you'd refuse to talk to me. I thought if I could get to know you, I could figure out a way to persuade you to meet your mother, talk to her."

"Persuade?" she repeated incredulously. "I've wanted to meet my mother my entire life! Dreamed that some day she and my father would realize they'd made a mistake and demand the Morans give me back. You didn't need to *persuade* me. All you had to do was ask."

Groaning, he sank down on the edge of the bed and covered his face with his hands. "I didn't know. None of us did. When Mom and Eddie went to see the Morans in hopes of finding you, they claimed you wanted nothing to do with them. They said you wanted us to leave you alone." He lifted his head to look at her. "I hated you for that. For hurting my stepmother. Eddie and Jase were going to track you down anyway, but Barbara refused to let them. Made them promise they would honor your wishes. That's why I came."

"And you slept with me," she said angrily. "How could you make love with me, and not tell me who you were, what you knew about me? That you knew my parents, my brother?"

He met her gaze in silence, wishing like hell he'd told her from the beginning who he was, why he was there, and knowing there was nothing he could say now that would excuse what he'd done, no words he could offer that would earn him her forgiveness.

She turned away, and began throwing clothes into the bag again. "I'm going home."

"Ali. You can't."

She laughed, the sound so bitter, so filled with futility it nearly broke his heart. "Oh. Right. I don't have a home to go to anymore."

"That's not what I meant," he said in frustration. "It's not safe for you to go there."

"Fine." She slammed the lid down on her bag and zipped it closed. "Then I'll go to Traci's." She grabbed her bag and headed for the door. "I'll be safe at her house. Whoever wants you dead won't know to look for me there. And I'm taking the rental car—it's in my name anyway. You, Mr. Zillionaire, can find your own way back from wherever you came from."

He stood in the bedroom of the cabin and watched her go, knowing he had no right to ask her to stay and knowing there was nothing he could say that would change anything even if he did.

Ali paced around Traci's kitchen, one hand clamped over her mouth to hold back the tears.

Dropping her hand, she whirled to face her friend. "It was all a huge lie! And I fell for it *and* him!"

"But why did he keep his identity from you?" Traci asked in confusion. "Why not just tell you he knew your family?"

"Because he didn't think I wanted to meet my birth parents. None of them did."

"Well, that's just crazy. Why would anyone think a thing like that?"

"Because, my parents, my *adoptive* parents," she clarified, "told them I didn't."

"That still doesn't explain why Garrett didn't tell you who he was."

"He thought if I knew, I'd refuse to talk to him." Tears welled in her eyes. "I slept with him!" she cried. "Can you imagine how that makes me feel? Knowing that meant nothing to him and everything to me?"

Ali dropped down on a chair. "It doesn't matter," she said wearily. "Not anymore." She dragged in a shuddery breath, forcing her thoughts away from Garrett.

"I have a brother, Traci," she said, still unable to believe it herself. "A twin brother." Fresh tears welled. "And I'll probably never see him again."

Traci sank down beside her and draped an arm around her shoulders. "Don't talk like that," she scolded. "You'll see him again."

"You weren't there," Ali said miserably. "It was such a shock. I screamed at him. All of them. Refused to believe him until he showed me his birth certificate."

"Of course you were shocked," Traci soothed. "If the situation were reversed, I'm sure he would've reacted the same way. Give yourself some time. Once you've had a chance to absorb all this, you can call him, meet the rest of your family."

"No, I can't," Ali said tearfully.

Traci gave her a reassuring squeeze. "Sure you can. You're just feeling a bit overwhelmed right now."

"Don't you understand?" Ali cried in frustration. "I can't meet them. Not with Garrett a part of their lives."

"Now that's just plain ridiculous," Traci lectured firmly. "Just because he's your mother's stepson doesn't mean you can't have a relationship with your parents."

"It would mean seeing him, hearing about him." She shook her head. "I couldn't bear it. It would hurt too much."

Traci's eyes slowly rounded. "You're in love with him?"

Ali started to shake her head in denial, then dropped her chin and nodded, tears streaming down her face.

"Oh, Ali," Traci murmured.

They sat in silence a moment, then Traci stood abruptly. "Well, you may be willing to toss away your chance to meet your family, but I'm not letting you. We're calling Jase. You deserve to know the details about your birth, to meet your parents. And if you're worried about bumping into Garrett, Jase can come here. I'll be right here with you. A buffer, if you feel you need one." She leveled a finger at Ali's nose. "But we are calling him. I'm not going to let Garrett Miller rob you of the chance to meet your family. You have as much right to be a part of their lives as he does. Maybe even more."

* * *

Traci bulldozed Ali into making the call to Jase and a meeting was arranged to take place two days later.

Even though Traci knew what time Jase and Mandy were expected to arrive, when the doorbell sounded, she shot off the sofa as if catapulted from it.

"They're here," she said, stating the obvious, then turned and gave Ali a quick hug of reassurance. "Now don't worry," she said nervously. "I'll be right here with you the whole time. If your brother or sister-in-law say or do anything that upsets you, just give me the word, and I'll personally kick them out the door."

Ali forced a smile for Traci's benefit. "Thanks. Hopefully that won't be necessary."

As Traci went to let their visitors in, Ali rose, wiping her damp palms down the sides of her legs.

Mandy entered the living room first and as soon as Ali saw the woman who had been so kind to her, tears surged to her eyes.

"Oh, Ali," Mandy cried, her face crumpling. She rushed across the room to throw her arms around Ali. "I'm so sorry," she said tearfully. "This is all such a mess."

Ali nodded, too choked by emotion for a moment to speak. "Yes, it is."

Mandy withdrew and caught Ali's hands, gave them a squeeze. "We're going to get this all straightened out, I promise." She turned to her husband. "Aren't we, Jase?"

He stepped forward and laid a hand on Ali's shoulder. "I damn sure hope so. I've been without a sister long enough."

After talking with Jase and Mandy for over an hour, Ali had even more questions to wonder about.

"And you say the Morans never gave you a letter from our mother?" Jase asked.

She shook her head. "No. And I would've remembered if they had. I asked about my birth parents a number of times, but they told me it was a private adoption and they knew nothing about them. When I was a teenager, fifteen or sixteen, I think, I tried to find them on my own. All I had to go on was what little information was on the birth certificate. I called the hospital and they told me they couldn't help me, that I would have to contact whatever lawyer was involved." She shrugged. "I had no idea who that was, so I gave up."

"Mom wrote you a letter," Jase assured her. "Same as she did me. She told me so. She even taped a piece of a deed on the back that was given to her by Eddie, our father. I have the other half."

Ali frowned. "Piece of a deed?"

"That's a story all by itself," Mandy interjected. "The night before he left for Vietnam, Eddie was in a bar with a bunch of other soldiers. They had a drink with a rancher and he wrote out a deed to his ranch, tore it into six pieces and gave each of the soldiers a piece, telling them to join the pieces together when they returned from Vietnam, and he would give them his ranch."

Ali's eyebrows shot up. "Are you kidding? He just gave them his ranch?"

"He was a widower," Jase explained, taking up the telling of the story. "His only son was killed in Vietnam. Eddie seems to think the rancher knew they were scared, knew what dangers they were going to face, and he was giving them a reason to survive the war and make it home."

"He gave them his ranch?" Ali said, finding it hard to believe that a complete stranger would do such a thing.

"So it seems," Jase said with a shrug. "All the pieces have been accounted for except Eddie's. He gave his to Mom and asked her to keep it for him until after the war. When she found out she was pregnant, she tried to contact Eddie, but was told he'd died in battle. They gave her the wrong information," he was quick to tell her. "He was injured, not killed. Anyway, with Mom thinking he was dead, when she learned she was carrying twins, she decided to put us up for adoption. I think you can understand her reasoning. A single woman left to raise a set of twins on her own? She was scared, grieving, afraid she wouldn't be able to properly care for us and thought she could insure us a better life if she gave us up.

"She wrote a letter to each of us. All she had of Eddie's was the piece of deed he'd given her, so she tore it in half and taped a piece to each of the letters, wanting us to have something that was his." He opened his hands. "We've already told you how I came to find my piece, as well as our parents."

"You mentioned visiting my parents," Ali began.

"The Doctors Scary?" He shuddered. "Sorry, but those are the coldest, most unfriendly people I've ever had the displeasure to meet."

"Jase!" Mandy cried, horrified that he might have offended Ali.

Hiding a smile, Ali patted Mandy's hand. "It's true. His description is right-on."

Somewhat mollified, Mandy released a breath, but gave Jase a warning look anyway.

"They didn't tell us anything," Jase went on to explain. "At least not how to find you. All they told us was that you wanted nothing to do with your birth family."

"And you believed them," she said, remembering Garrett had told her the same thing.

Jase opened his hands. "Why wouldn't we? We didn't particularly care for the Morans, but we had no reason to think they'd lie." He shook his head sadly. "Mom, she took it real hard. Dad and I were prepared to turn the world upside down until we found you, but Mom put her foot down. Said we had to respect your right for privacy and made us promise we'd leave you alone." He scowled. "Unfortunately she didn't include Garrett in that promise-making."

"He meant well," Mandy said in Garrett's defense. "He's very close to Barbara. Overly protective, at times. It made him mad that you wouldn't agree to meet her."

When Ali opened her mouth to deny her unwillingness, Mandy held up a hand. "That's what he thought, anyway. What we *all* thought." She lifted a shoulder. "Anyway, that's why he decided to play detective." She rolled her eyes. "Not a very smart move on his part, but his heart was in the right place."

Ali released a breath. "If you don't mind," she said, "I'd rather we not talk about him."

Jase and Mandy exchanged a look.

"So?" Jase said, and clapped his hands against his thighs. "When do you want to meet Mom and Dad?"

Ali didn't know how to respond. Jase's and Mandy's expectant and hopeful expressions indicated their desire for her to agree to an immediate date, but a voice inside her cried for caution. What if she agreed to meet her parents and, for whatever reason, they chose not to be a part of her life? She'd had her heart bruised by her adoptive parents so many times in the past, she was hesitant to expose herself to hurt again.

Plus, there was Garrett to consider. Agreeing to meet her parents would surely mean seeing him again, and she wasn't prepared for that. Not yet.

Refusing to be forced into committing to something, she gave an honest, if nonanswer. "I need to think about this. There's more to consider here than just meeting my birth parents."

Jase's disappointment was almost palpable.

Mandy's was just as obvious, but was quickly masked behind a kind smile.

"There's no hurry," she assured Ali. "Barbara and Eddie will understand your hesitation. Take whatever time you need and give us a call when you're ready."

With nothing left for any of them to say, Jase stood. "Thank you for inviting us to come and talk with you," he said to Ali, then turned to Traci. "And you for allowing us the use of your home."

Ali stood, as well. "I—" She stopped, suddenly overcome with emotion, as if she were saying goodbye to them for the last time. "I'm sorry," she said, pressing a finger beneath her nose. "I…this has all been so upsetting."

To her surprise, Jase gathered her up in his arms and gave her a tight tug. "This isn't goodbye," he said as if reading her mind. "We're going to be seeing a lot of each other." He pushed her out to arm's length to smile down at her. "Hell, we're almost neighbors. San Saba's not that far a drive from here."

She stared up at him, realizing this was his way of telling her he'd still be a part of her life, no matter what decision she made about their parents. Tears filled her eyes, joy her heart. "No, San Saba's not far, at all."

Jase reached for Mandy's hand and turned to leave, then snapped his fingers and turned back around. "I almost forgot. Garrett asked me to tell you it's safe for you to go back home."

Ali wasn't sure what she'd expected to feel upon returning to the Vista after staying with Traci a week, but it certainly wasn't the sense of gloom that engulfed her as she walked through rooms that had brought her such joy and comfort for more than ten years.

She blamed her melancholy on the house being sold, on her being forced to move and leave the home she loved behind. But she knew in her heart that wasn't the cause. The root of her sadness was the man who had shared the house with her for a short space of time. Everywhere she looked she saw Garrett. Sitting at the bar in the kitchen eating his breakfast. Sprawled on the sofa in the den, watching *Jeopardy*.

Even her private quarters offered no refuge. The scent of sandalwood she would always associate with Garrett hung in the air, a constant reminder of the night he'd "chosen" her bed to sleep in. And when she curled up in her bed at night to sleep, she envisioned him there, braced above her, as he'd been the night she'd awakened him to tell him about the men she'd seen lurking outside.

She tried telling herself she hadn't fallen in love with him. What she'd felt for him was an infatuation that any woman might have experienced upon finding herself in the company of a man of such wealth and stature. But she knew that wasn't the case. As foolish as it was, she had fallen in love with him. With a man who had as little respect for her feelings and needs as the people who had raised her. A man who had deceived her and withheld information for his own gain.

So she did what she always did in times of strife. She mentally boxed up her sadness and disappointments and filed them away, refusing to give them credence, and went about the task of packing what belongings she'd gathered in the span of ten years.

And if she had to pause and wipe away an occasional tear as she went along, she blamed it on allergies or the dust she was stirring. It certainly wasn't because she was missing Garrett.

Eight

"So he's behind bars?" Garrett asked his security chief, Joe.

"Currently in Switzerland, but the Feds are in negotiations to have him transferred to the United States. Since he committed no crime in their country, the Swiss shouldn't have a problem releasing him to us."

Garrett shook his head, still unable to believe the man who'd made his life a living hell for the last three months was no longer a threat.

"Were you able to talk to him?" he asked Joe.

"Briefly. A more extensive interrogation will take place once we have him back in the States."

"Did he say why he wanted to kill me?"

Joe rolled his ever-present toothpick to the far corner of his mouth and averted his gaze, as if hesitant to share what he knew.

"It was me he wanted dead," Garrett reminded him.

"It was at that," Joe said, and with a sigh, laid out what facts he'd managed to pull from the man. "Jealousy and greed is what it boiled down to," he said in summation. "You had everything, and he wanted it."

"But why me?" Garrett asked in frustration. "There are others with more money who make themselves easier targets."

"But not a one of them went to the same high school you did."

"High school?" Garrett repeated. "He's someone I know?"

Joe shrugged again. "Don't know whether you do or not. The name's Matt Collins."

Garrett frowned, trying to put the name with a face, then shook his head. "Never heard of him."

"He knew you, all right. Had his eye on you for years, the hate building as he watched you get richer and richer. Thought himself smarter than you, deserved what you had. Worked as a tech for the company a couple years back. Got fired for stealing equipment. Since then he's moved from job to job, biding his time, waiting for the opportunity." He pulled the now shredded toothpick from his mouth and tossed it into the leather wastebasket beside the desk. "He walked right into the trap, oblivious to what was going on around him."

"What about the guy who doubled for me? Was he hurt?"

"Not a scratch on him. We sprang the trap before the perp could snatch him."

Garrett wondered how many times he'd been within the man's reach and never known it, then shook off the thought, knowing he couldn't allow himself to think like that and hope to lead any kind of normal life in the future.

He stood and extended a hand across the desk. "I appreciate all you did, Joe. I owe you my life."

Joe rose and clasped his hand, shook. "Just doing my job."

Garrett waited until the door closed behind Joe, then seated himself again behind his desk and reached for the mail he was reviewing when Joe had arrived with his report.

Noticing a padded envelope, he pulled it from the stack, but froze when he saw the familiar logo of the Vista Bed and Breakfast. Noticing his hand had begun to shake, he flexed his fingers a couple of times, before opening the envelope. He peered inside, then pulled out the bundle of photographs enclosed.

A slip of paper clipped to the bundle read: "Souvenir pictures from your trip to Texas, as promised," and was signed with an "A."

He stared at the note a moment, then swore and picked up the phone and punched in the number for the Vista, telling himself it was ridiculous to continue on this way. He listened through four rings before the recorder clicked on.

"You've reached the Vista Bed and Breakfast. I'm sorry I can't take your call right now. Please leave your name and number and I'll call you back as soon as I can."

He held the phone to his ear another moment, just to make sure she didn't pick up, then returned it to its cradle when it became obvious she wasn't going to answer. Scooping up the pictures from his desk, he leaned back in his chair.

How would she categorize this series of shots? he wondered as he thumbed through the pictures. Theme or story? There was only him in each frame, but he didn't recall her saying the number of subjects assigned it to any particular category. He paused at the picture of him standing with one boot braced on the boulder, and chuckled, remembering Ali's instructions.

Give me a forlorn look. You know. Like you've been running from the law for months, and you're missing that pretty little saloon girl you met up in Dodge City.

His smile slowly faded. If she wanted forlorn, she should see him now, he thought. If missing a girl produced the look, he sure as hell qualified, because he missed Ali in the worst sort of way.

Scowling, he sat up and tossed the pictures to the desk. Too bad she didn't feel the same, he thought as he eyed the single line of handwriting on the note clipped to the pictures. No, "Hi, how are you," or, better yet, "Can we hit Rewind?" the phrase she'd used when they'd gotten off to the bad start the day he'd arrived in Austin.

How he'd like to hit Rewind, he thought with regret. If he had it to do over again, he'd do things right.

He tensed, his brain snagging on the idea of a second chance. It was possible, he told himself. He'd agreed to hit Rewind when she'd asked it of him. Shouldn't she be required to do the same?

Losing your temper and deceiving someone doesn't exactly fall into the same "sin" category.

He scowled at his conscience's assessment of the situation. Okay, so she probably wouldn't give him a second chance.

Groaning, he dropped his head to his hands. Dammit, he missed her. Wanted to be with her. And if he was half as smart as people thought him, he would've told her he loved her when he had the chance.

He balled his hands into fists against his desk. There had to be a way to work this out, he thought in frustration. A way to make her understand why he'd done what he'd done, convince her to give him another chance.

The obvious was simply getting his butt back to Texas and asking her for that chance. But he couldn't just show up on her doorstep. What would he say? More, what would *she* say when she saw him? He choked a breath. Hell, that was a no-brainer. She'd slam the door in his face.

No, he had to have a purpose, a reason for going to her house. And he was going to have to come up with one pretty darn quick, because she wouldn't be living at the Vista much longer. Not if Ronald Fleming had his way.

He tensed at the reminder of Ronald Fleming. That's it! he thought, and pushed from his chair.

She couldn't refuse to let Garrett into a house he *owned!*

Throughout the flight home to Austin, Ali kept waiting for a delayed reaction to set in. Anger. Regret. Loss. But she felt nothing. She supposed she shouldn't have expected to feel anything after confronting her adoptive parents with all she'd learned about her birth family. She certainly had no regrets. Those she would reserve for her parents, although she was sure they considered themselves beyond fault. As to loss, how could she mourn something she'd never truly had? Her adoptive parents had never loved her, and whatever feelings she might've had for them they'd frozen out of her years ago.

As she pulled up to the front gate of the Vista and waited for the electronic gate to open, she noticed a bright red Sold banner had been added to the For Sale sign during her absence. The regret and loss she had expected to feel after the ugly confrontation with her parents filled her throat. But she felt no anger. She couldn't be mad at Claire's father for taking something that was never hers to begin with.

Blinking back tears, she drove through the gate and parked in front of the house. Gathering her tote from the passenger seat, she climbed from the car and walked to the front door. Rather than dig for her house key, she punched the code into the keyless entry, turned the knob and stepped into the house she'd thought of as home for more than ten years.

She set her tote on the floor beside the mahogany hall tree, and looked around as she shrugged out of her coat. Open boxes sat on the living room floor, packed with the carefully wrapped treasures she'd collected over the years. White sheets draped the tapestry sofas Mimi had left behind. Gulping back emotion, she hung her coat over one of the hall tree's brass hooks and headed for the den and her stereo, anxious to push back the oppressive silence with the sound of music.

She flipped through her stack of CDs, selected a disc of hits from the sixties, seventies and eighties and slid it into the player. With Mick Jagger and The Rolling Stones grinding out "Ruby Tuesday," she turned for the kitchen.

And jerked to a stop, just managing to squelch the scream that shot to her throat. Garrett stood at the foot of the rear staircase, dressed in the jeans, boots and Western shirt she'd picked out for him. She stared, her heart threatening to break.

That he would have the nerve to enter her home after what he'd done to her, filled her with fury. "What are you doing here?"

"Taking care of some unfinished business."

Which told her absolutely nothing. "How did you get in?"

"Used the code you gave me. Still works."

Silently cursing herself for not thinking to change it, she folded her arms across her chest. "The Vista is closed. You'll have to find someplace else to stay."

"You're here," he said, stating the obvious.

"I *live* here," she reminded him tersely, then remembered the Sold sign out front and added, "for the time being, anyway."

"I paid for a month and stayed here considerably less than that. I'm due a few days."

She dropped her hands into fists at her sides, angry with him for coming here unannounced, for opening a wound she was praying would eventually heal. "Why are you doing this, Garrett? You can afford to stay anywhere you want. Why insist upon staying *here?*"

"I told you," he said, and started toward her. "I'm due a few days yet."

"Fine," she said, and whirled for the writing desk where she kept the books for the Vista. "I'll refund your money." She snatched open the lap drawer, yanked out the checkbook, then dropped down on the chair. "You were here, what? Two weeks? I'll refund half your money."

"I don't want a refund. I want to stay."

She flinched at the nearness of his voice, unaware that he'd moved to stand behind her. Setting her jaw, she pressed the pen to the check and began filling it out. "Well, you're not. The Vista's closed."

"As I recall, it was closed when you agreed to take my reservations for the month of January."

"Yes," she said tersely. "It was always closed in January. That's when I took my vacation."

"What's the difference? Closed is closed, right?"

She slammed the pen down and spun on the chair to look up at him. It was a mistake. But certainly not the first she'd made concerning Garrett Miller.

His brown eyes seemed to grab her, holding her captive. She squeezed her own eyes shut to block whatever power it was he had over her. "I don't want you here."

"Why?"

She flipped open her eyes to glare at him. "Because I don't. Okay?" She spun back around and quickly finished filling out the check, tore it from the book. Pushing to her feet, she thrust it at him. "Take your money and go."

"Could we hit Rewind?"

"What?" she said incredulously.

"Hit Rewind. I seem to have gotten off on the wrong foot with you."

She closed her eyes again, gulped, then opened them to meet his gaze, sure that he was determined to rip her heart right out of her chest. "Don't. Please. Just go."

He lifted a hand and swept her hair back from her face. "Now that doesn't seem quite fair. When you asked me if we could hit Rewind, I didn't refuse you."

The tears welled higher, the pain in her chest so strong she was afraid it would drag her to her knees. "Garrett. Please."

He tucked the lock of hair behind her ear and sidled closer. "Please, what, Ali?"

She gulped, swallowed. "Please, don't hurt me anymore."

"I won't. Not intentionally. I never meant to hurt you before."

"But you did. You lied to me."

He slipped his arms around her waist. "I didn't lie. I just didn't tell you the whole truth."

She pressed her hands against his chest, fighting the urge to melt into his arms, knowing she couldn't resume the relationship they had before, if that's what he wanted. Not when she knew now that she loved him.

"You slept with me," she cried. "Made love with me. How could you do that and know what you knew, and not tell me?" She curled her hands into fists against his chest, the tears a stream of fire streaking down her face. "What was I? A nice diversion for you, while you waited for the perfect opportunity to get what you wanted from me?

"I made love with you because I wanted you, Garrett. *You.* I even fell in love with you. I didn't mean to, and if I had it to do over, I'd do everything within my power to keep from loving you." She swept a frustrated hand over her cheeks, furious with herself for baring her soul to him, letting him see how much he meant to her. "I can't undo what's done. But I *can* protect my heart from any more hurt. I lived my whole life trying to win my parents' love and they couldn't or wouldn't love me back. I won't go through that again. I can't."

"I wouldn't want you to," he said softly. He stroked his fingers along her cheek, watching their movement, before shifting his gaze back to hers. "Feelings don't come easy for me. And I'm not saying that to excuse the way I treated you. I spent the first six years of my life without affection. Never truly experienced anything close to it until my stepmother came into my life. Even then it was hard for me to show my feelings, harder to express them."

He cupped a hand at her cheek. "But I do love you, Ali. As hard as you might find that to believe, I love you with all my heart."

She pressed a hand to her lips, her gaze fixed on his. "Oh, Garrett," she whispered. "I didn't know. I thought—"

He hugged her hard against his chest. "I know. You thought I had used you, deceived you, and I understand why you would feel that way. I handled all this poorly from the beginning. Before coming to Austin I had already made up my mind to dislike you." He drew his head back to look down at her. "I believed you had hurt my stepmother, the one person in my life who cared about me. When I came here, it was for her. I wanted her to be happy, and I knew she wouldn't be until she had the opportunity to see you, talk to you, explain to you why she had given you up." He laid a hand against her cheek. "And maybe I wanted revenge, to hurt you as much as you had hurt her. But that was all before I met you, got to know you. Before I realized you were the victim, not the villain I'd thought you to be."

"Oh, Garrett," she said tearfully. "My parents

should have never told her that. When I read the letter she wrote me—"

"You read the letter?" he said in confusion.

She nodded.

"But I thought you said you'd never gotten a letter?"

"I hadn't. Not until yesterday."

"But…where? How?"

"I flew up to see my parents and asked for it."

He turned her toward the sofa and urged her down, sat beside her. "They had the letter all this time and never gave it to you?"

She dropped her gaze and shook her head. "No. In fact, Mother denied having it until I told her I'd seen Jase's letter and knew that my birth mother had written one to me, too. I asked her about my birth certificate, too. Why it had single birth listed, when Jase's was marked as being a twin." She looked up at him, unable to hide the hurt. "She did it. Mother." She shook her head again, still unable to believe her mother would go to such lengths. "She'd never admit it, but I think she was afraid I'd try to find my birth parents. That's why she never gave me the letter."

"And you read all of it?"

She nodded. "During the flight home." Tears welled in her eyes. "I wish so badly I'd had it years ago. She loved me, Garrett. Even though she gave me up, she loved me. I could feel it in every word she wrote, and I felt her pain. I can't even imagine how hard it was for her to make the decision to give me up for adoption."

"She wanted what was best for you. You and Jase."

She smiled sadly. "I know that now. I just wish I'd known it years ago. Maybe it would've made living with my parents a little easier."

"Would you like to meet her?"

"More than anything. My father, too."

A broad smile spread across his face. "That can be arranged. But first—" He leaned back and dug a hand into his pocket. "This is for you."

She frowned in confusion at the key he offered her. "What's this?"

"The key to the Vista."

She choked a laugh. "Thanks," she said and pushed his hand away. "But I won't be needing a key to the Vista much longer."

He nudged the key against her hand, urging her to take it. "No, it's yours."

"I don't understand."

"It's yours. The Vista. I bought it."

Her jaw sagged. "You bought the Vista?"

"Signed the papers first thing this morning."

"But…why?"

"Since I'm planning on building a satellite location here, I figure we'll need a place to stay when we're in town."

"Garrett," she said, afraid she'd misunderstood. "What are you saying?"

He shook his head sadly. "I guess I've handled this as poorly as I did reuniting you with your mother." He closed his hand around hers. "I want you to marry me, Ali. I know how much you love this house, and I'd never ask you to give it up. We can split our time between D.C. and Austin. Or, if you'd prefer, this can be our permanent residence, and I'll keep my house in D.C. for when I need to be there on business."

"Wait," she said weakly. "Back up to that part about you wanting to marry me."

Laughing, he wrapped his arms around her and hugged her tight. "That's one of the things I love most about you, Ali. You don't have a clue how irresistible I find you."

She clung to him, as if he were a mirage that would disappear if she dared let go. "I can't believe this. Me, Ali Moran, marrying a zillionaire."

"I'd worry if I thought it was my money you were after."

She jerked back to look at him in alarm. "I swear it's you I love, not your money."

Smiling, he drew her back into his arms. "And that's another thing I like about you. You'd be as happy poor as you would be rich."

"Uh, Garrett." She pulled back to look at him. "That's not exactly true. I've been broke before, and I really don't want to ever be that way again."

"And you won't be," he assured her. "I'll always take care of you. Always."

Tears filled her eyes at his promise, and she leaned to press her lips to his. "And I'll always take care of you."

"Ah, Ali," he said, hugging her tight. "I love you so much."

"And I love you."

He set her aside. "Now about meeting your mother," he said and stood.

She sputtered a laugh. "What are you going to do? Make me sign a pledge, or something?"

"No, I'm going to get her." He turned toward the rear staircase. "Mom? Eddie? You can come down now."

Ali's eyes went as round as saucers as she heard the pounding of feet overhead. "They're here?" she said in disbelief.

Smiling proudly, he nodded. "Just waiting for me to pop the question before they came down to meet you."

She shot to her feet. "Now?" she cried, and began scrubbing at her cheeks and finger-combing her hair. "But look at me. I'm a mess!"

Garrett caught her hands and brought them to his lips. "No, you're not. You're beautiful."

"Oh, you're just saying that," she chided, then froze, her eyes going wide, as a man and woman appeared at the foot of the staircase.

The woman spoke first, her voice, as well as her posture hesitant. "Ali?"

Ali couldn't speak. The resemblance to herself

was so strong, she knew she was looking at her mother. She placed a hand at her throat, nodded. "Y-yes. I'm Ali." She took a tentative step, another, then was running across the room and throwing her arms around her mother.

"Well, I'll be a son-of-a-gun," Eddie said, swiping a tear from his eye. "She looks just like you, Barbara."

Barbara pushed Ali back to hold at arm's length, so that she could look at her. "Oh, no, Eddie," she said softly. "She's beautiful. Our daughter is absolutely beautiful."

She reached for Garrett's hand and drew him to join the circle, she, her husband Eddie and their daughter formed.

"My family is complete now," she said, her smile radiant. "Eddie, the babies we lost so many years ago, and the son of my heart, Garrett."

Turning her face up to Garrett, she gave his hand a squeeze. "If I'd been given the charge of choosing a wife for you, or choosing a husband for my daughter, I couldn't have found a more perfect match for either of you, or one I could love any more than I do the two of you."

Late that same night, Ali lay in her bed, unable to sleep for thinking about all that happened that day. In the span of a few short hours, she'd become engaged, had the key to the Vista presented to her and met her birth parents. It was a wonder she wasn't doing cartwheels down the street!

She heard the squeak of her bedroom door opening and sat up. "Garrett?" she whispered uncertainly.

"Who were you expecting?" he teased as he climbed into bed with her.

She shot a nervous glance up at the ceiling. "What if Barbara and Eddie heard you?"

"Don't worry. I was quiet as a mouse."

Smothering a laugh, she cuddled up next to him. "I feel like a teenager sneaking around behind her parents' back."

He slipped a hand beneath her pajama top and cupped her breast. "Kind of adds an element of excitement, doesn't it?"

"I'm not sure I can take much more excitement," she said breathlessly.

Smiling, he pressed his lips to hers. "I love you, Ali."

She laid a hand against his cheek. "I'll never get tired of hearing you say that." She slipped her arms around his neck. "Make love with me, Garrett," she whispered.

"What if Barbara or Eddie get up for a drink of water or something and hear us?"

She nipped at his ear. "I think they'll understand, don't you?"

Epilogue

Two years later....

Ali drew in a deep breath, savoring the scent of wild honeysuckle that filled the air.

"You okay?"

She glanced up to find Garrett looking at her, his brow furrowed in concern. Smiling, she hugged his arm to her side. "I'm fine. Just enjoying the fresh air. It's beautiful here, isn't it? So quiet and peaceful."

Garrett looked around at the tranquil setting they stood in, then turned his gaze to the memorial they'd come to unveil. "That was the hope when this was designed."

"Do you think they know?" she asked. "The soldiers, I mean. Do you think they somehow know the rancher honored his promise to them?"

"One of them does," he said, and tipped his head toward Eddie, who stood on the fringe of the group gathered, his gaze on the statue of the six soldiers. "Your dad."

She blinked back tears, still finding it hard to believe that after all these years, her dream of being united with her birth family had become a reality.

"I can't imagine how he must feel," she said, "knowing he's the only one of the soldiers to make it to this day."

"I imagine he's experiencing a lot of different emotions at the moment. Pride. Sadness. Joy."

She looked at him curiously. "Joy?"

"Think about it. For over thirty years, Eddie lived a solitary life, thinking he'd lost the woman he loved and unaware he'd fathered a set of twins. Now he and Barbara are married, and he not only has a son and a daughter, but a son- and daughter-in-law, as well."

A toddler waddled up and stretched up her hands to Garrett. "Hol' me."

"And grandchildren, too," he added, chuckling, then reached down and swung his niece up into his arms. She immediately laid her head on his shoulder and popped her thumb into her mouth. "Hey, sunshine," he said. "Are you sleepy?"

"Uh-uh," she said, even as her eyes shuttered close. "Molly no take nap."

Hiding a smile, Ali slipped her arm around Garrett's waist. "You're going to make a wonderful father."

He lifted a brow. "You think so?"

"I know so. Molly's a hard-sell and she thinks you're fabulous."

"That's because she has me wrapped around her finger. All she has to do is bat those pretty blue eyes at me, and I'll do whatever she wants."

Ali laid a hand over her swollen stomach. "If you're that big a sucker for little girls, let's hope we have boys."

Garrett released a shuddery breath. "Twins. I'm still having a hard time wrapping my mind around the idea of us having two babies, instead of just one."

"Better get used to it," she warned. "They'll be here sooner than you think. Oh, look," she said, spotting a couple making their way up the path to the memorial. "There's Stephanie and Wade Parker."

"The lady responsible for starting all this. That's Wade's daughter with them, isn't it?" he said, straining to see who was following the couple.

"Yes, that's Heather." Ali laughed softly. "And

that's their son Clayton Heather's pulling in the wagon. Isn't he a doll?"

"Better not let Wade hear you refer to his son as a 'doll,'" Garrett warned. "Men are funny like that. Always worrying women are going to turn their sons into sissies."

"And women are afraid men are going to spoil their daughters and turn them into prima donnas."

Smiling, Garrett pressed a kiss to Molly's cheek. "Hard not to spoil someone who's so darn cute."

"Have you seen Leah Forrester?" she asked, as she searched the crowd.

"Is she the one who's married to the Special Forces guy?"

"Yes. Sam. Though he's no longer in the military."

"I saw them a minute ago over by the pavilion, checking on the arrangements for the dinner we're having later."

"That woman is an organizational wonder. I can't imagine organizing an affair for a group of this size."

Out of the corner of her eye she saw her father, Eddie, begin to make his way toward the podium, and eased closer to Garrett. "I think the service is about to start," she whispered.

As Eddie stepped onto the flatbed trailer that was serving as their dais, quiet settled over the crowd.

Emotion swelled in Ali's throat, as she watched him walk toward the podium, his head up, his shoulders square, knowing he was concentrating hard on his gait, to hide the limp the war had left him with. When he reached the podium, Ali laced her fingers through Garrett's and squeezed.

"My name is Eddie Davis," he said into the microphone. He turned to look behind him at the statue of the six soldiers. "And I'd like to introduce you to some of my friends." He lifted a hand. "That guy in the middle there," he said, pointing. "That's Poncho. He's the only one of the six who doesn't have family representing him here today. Poncho chose a different road to travel, but he was a good soldier and a good friend.

"The guy to the left of Poncho is Preacher. A kinder person, or one with a more generous heart, you'll never meet." He gestured again. "And next to Preacher is T.J. For years, T.J. was listed as Missing in Action, but thanks to the work of Sam Forrester and his team of Special Forces, T.J.'s classification was recently changed to Killed in Action, which allowed his family to finally lay him to rest.

"If you'll look to the right of Poncho, that's Romeo." He laughed softly. "Now, Romeo knew how to romance a woman, no doubt about it, which is how he came by the nickname. But Romeo had a natural friendliness and spirit of fun that surpassed gender and made him a favorite with everyone he met.

"That ugly devil to the right of Romeo—" he

chuckled "—well, that's me." His smile faded, and he blew out a shuddery breath. "And I'm here to tell you, it feels mighty strange to be looking at a memorial statue of myself and still be standing here breathing."

Laughter rippled through the crowd. When it subsided, Eddie gestured again, pointing to the statue on the far right. "And that tall, lanky man is Pops. If you'll notice, the artist who created the memorial placed Pops' statue where it appears he's walking a half-step or so behind the others, his eyes cut to the right, as if he's keeping an eye on the others."

He paused a moment, gulped, then turned to face the audience. "There's a reason for that. Pops trained us, looked after us, kept us in line. Kicked our tails, when he thought we needed it. Most importantly he loved us." He paused again, to drag the back of his hand across his eyes. "Pops tried his damnedest to take care of us, get us all home alive." He shook his head sadly. "But some things just weren't meant to be."

He glanced back at the statues. "Each of these six men represents thousands of other soldiers just like him. Men, who were willing to put their lives on the line for their country in the fight for freedom."

He held up a hand, as if staving off an argument. "Now I know there are those who hate war and are constantly protesting for peace. And there are those who think we shouldn't be honoring soldiers who, in their eyes, are the same as murderers. But you know what? Not a one of these six men started that war. They did what was asked of them, what was expected of them. For some, it meant making the ultimate sacrifice. Their lives. For others, like me, it meant losing a foot, or a limb."

He gripped his hands on the sides of the podium and leaned forward, his gaze intense. "There was one man who appreciated the sacrifices our soldiers were asked to make and that was Walt Webber. In a bar more than thirty years ago, Mr. Webber wrote out a deed and gave each of us soldiers portrayed here a piece of that paper, telling us to join those pieces when we returned and take ownership of his ranch.

"Some say Mr. Webber was crazy, that the loss of his own son in Vietnam had driven him over the edge. There are others who say he never intended to give his ranch to a bunch of strangers. Whether there is any truth in that statement, I don't know, but I do know this. When Walt Webber looked into the faces of those six soldiers that night, he saw youth and he saw fear. He'd lost a son in the same war we were going to fight, and like any father, he wanted to do something to alleviate that fear. He wanted to give us a reason to stay alive, to make it home. So he signed his ranch over to us and gave each of us a piece of the deed to keep."

Eddie dug into his pocket, pulled out the faded

piece of paper and held it up for all to see. "This is the piece that Walt Webber gave to me that night. To some of you, it may look like nothing more than a scrap of trash, but to me, it represented hope, one man's belief that I'd make it home one day."

He laid the piece of paper on the podium, then lifted his gaze to the audience again. "I'm proud of you," he said, speaking directly to the children of the soldiers. "I'm proud of what you've done to make this day possible. You believed when others doubted. You persisted when others would've given up. You persevered when faced with seemingly insurmountable problems. As a group, you made the decision to take Walt Webber's ranch and turn it into a sanctuary and retreat for *all* veterans, not just the ones it was originally given to. In creating this place, you honor not only the memory of the soldiers memorialized here, but the memory of Mr. Webber and his son, as well."

He braced a hand on the podium and turned to look at the statues. "T.J. Preacher. Poncho. Romeo. Pops. I've never forgotten a one of you boys." He dragged an arm across his eyes, clearing the moisture from them. "And I never will."

* * * * *

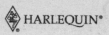

® HARLEQUIN®

INTRIGUE®

BREATHTAKING ROMANTIC SUSPENSE

Look for

UNDER
HIS SKIN

BY RITA HERRON

Nurse Grace Gardener brought
Detective Parker Kilpatrick back from
the brink of death, only to seek his
protection. On a collision course with
two killers who want to keep their
secrets, she's recruited the one detective
with the brass to stop them.

Available February wherever you buy books.

BECAUSE THE BEST PART
OF A GREAT ROMANCE
IS THE MYSTERY.

Texas Hold 'Em

When it comes to love, the stakes are high

Sixteen years ago, Luke Chisum dated
Becky Parker on a dare…before going
on to break her heart. Now the former
River Bluff daredevil is back, rekindling
desire and tempting Becky to pick up
where they left off. But this time she has
to resist or Luke could discover the secret
she's kept locked away all these years.…

Look for

TEXAS BLUFF

by Linda Warren

#1470

*Available February 2008
wherever you buy books.*

REQUEST YOUR FREE BOOKS!

2 FREE NOVELS PLUS 2 FREE GIFTS!

Silhouette®

Desire®

Passionate, Powerful, Provocative!

YES! Please send me 2 FREE Silhouette Desire® novels and my 2 FREE gifts. After receiving them, if I don't wish to receive any more books, I can return the shipping statement marked "cancel." If I don't cancel, I will receive 6 brand-new novels every month and be billed just $3.80 per book in the U.S., or $4.47 per book in Canada, plus 25¢ shipping and handling per book and applicable taxes, if any*. That's a savings of almost 15% off the cover price! I understand that accepting the 2 free books and gifts places me under no obligation to buy anything. I can always return a shipment and cancel at any time. Even if I never buy another book from Silhouette, the two free books and gifts are mine to keep forever.

225 SDN EEXJ   326 SDN EEXU

Name	(PLEASE PRINT)	
Address		Apt.
City	State/Prov.	Zip/Postal Code

Signature (if under 18, a parent or guardian must sign)

Mail to the **Silhouette Reader Service™**:
IN U.S.A.: P.O. Box 1867, Buffalo, NY 14240-1867
IN CANADA: P.O. Box 609, Fort Erie, Ontario L2A 5X3

Not valid to current Silhouette Desire subscribers.

Want to try two free books from another line?
Call 1-800-873-8635 or visit www.morefreebooks.com.

* Terms and prices subject to change without notice. NY residents add applicable sales tax. Canadian residents will be charged applicable provincial taxes and GST. This offer is limited to one order per household. All orders subject to approval. Credit or debit balances in a customer's account(s) may be offset by any other outstanding balance owed by or to the customer. Please allow 4 to 6 weeks for delivery.

Your Privacy: Silhouette is committed to protecting your privacy. Our Privacy Policy is available online at www.eHarlequin.com or upon request from the Reader Service. From time to time we make our lists of customers available to reputable firms who may have a product or service of interest to you. If you would prefer we not share your name and address, please check here. ☐

SDES07

is proud to present

Because sex doesn't have to be serious!

Don't miss the next red-hot title...

PRIMAL INSTINCTS
by
Jill Monroe

Ava Simms's sexual instincts take over as she puts her theories about mating to the test with gorgeous globe-traveling journalist Ian Cole. He's definitely up for the challenge—but is she?

On sale February 2008 wherever books are sold.

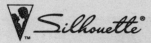

Silhouette®

Romantic
SUSPENSE

Sparked by Danger, Fueled by Passion.

When Tech Sergeant Jacob "Mako" Stone opens his door to a mysterious woman without a past, he knows his time off is over. As threats to Dee's life bring her and Jacob together, she must set aside her pride and accept the help of the military hero with too many secrets of his own.

Out of Uniform
by Catherine Mann

Available February wherever you buy books.

You can lead a horse to water...

When Alyssa Barkley and Clint Westmoreland
found out that their "fake" marriage was never
rendered void, they are forced to live together
for thirty days. However, Clint loves the single
life and has no intention of being tamed, but
when Alyssa moves in, the sizzling attraction
between them is ignited and neither wants the
thirty days to end.

Look for

TAMING CLINT
WESTMORELAND

by

BRENDA
JACKSON

Available February wherever you buy books

COMING NEXT MONTH